Ainsley St Claire

VENTURE CAPITALIST
Book 7

Longing

A Novel

Venture Capitalist: Longing/Ainsley St Claire—1st edition

ABOUT LONGING

She's a biotech researcher in race with time for a cure. If she pauses to have a life, will she lose the race?

Bella works horrific hours to find a cure for the disease that is killing her father. She doesn't have time for a social life or love. When a hacker threatens to tank the business, she turns to the one man she thinks can help. But, is he the one distraction she can't afford?

With his future riding on this deal, Christopher will pull out all the stops. But venture capital is all about risk and reward. He knows the reward of Bella is worth the risk to his job. When her life crumbles, he must somehow find a way to save her, regardless of the consequences.

As Bella and Christopher navigate illness, chaos, and a stalker, can they find the cure together?

Longing is book 8 in the sizzling Venture Capitalist romantic suspense series. If you like white-hot passion, burning mysteries, and smouldering bachelors, then you'll love Ainsley St Claire's steamy novel.

OTHER BOOKS BY AINSLEY ST CLAIRE

If you enjoy Longing, you might enjoy the other sensual, sexy and romantic stories and books she has published.

In a Perfect World

Venture Capitalist: Forbidden Love

Venture Capitalist: Promise

Venture Capitalist: Desire

Venture Capitalist: Temptation

Venture Capitalist: Obsession

Venture Capitalist: Flawless

Venture Capitalist: Longing
(June 2019)

Venture Capitalist: *Enchanted*
(July 2019)

Venture Capitalist: Fascination
(September 2019)

Venture Capitalist: Gifted
(November 2019)

chapter

ONE

ISABELLA

"Hey, chica!" Ellie, my best friend, says through the phone while I wrap up my day, hoping to get home soon. "You ready to go out tonight and party?"

"You know I'd love to go out with you and your latest boy toy. However, I really have this paper to finish by next week for peer review, plus grade papers from my students, in addition to all the work I need to get done for my paying job. The weekend will be short as it is, and we have someone coming in next week about investing, and I have a heavy role in that."

"Oh, come on, you can take one night off. It's going to be a girls' night out. No boy toys. You work 365 days a year. You can take a day off now and again."

"It's not that easy since I'm trying to get my PhD before I'm thirty-five while working full time, teaching classes at the university, and starting a company. I need to concentrate. I'll have plenty of time for fun when I graduate."

"Pretty please with a cherry on top? Please come out with me tonight? It's my birthday."

Guilt sits like a lead weight in my stomach. I should be with my best friend on her birthday. "Where are you thinking of going?"

"I was thinking about The Church. It's that new club in the Tenderloin neighborhood."

"Nice name. Do we go there to confess our sins?"

She giggles. "Maybe just to commit a few. Please? Will you come with me?"

She's wearing me down. I haven't been out in ages, and as my best friend, Ellie always supports me. I think about all the work I have to do and realize nothing is so important it can't wait until later. I can go for a short time. "Okay, fine. What time do you want to meet there?"

"Oh no, we're not going to meet you there. We're going to pick you up to make sure that you actually come and not fall into a book. Do you want to grab a bite first?"

"No. I really can't. I'm giving you three hours max."

"You can get your work done before we pick you up at your place at ten o'clock. Wear the shortest dress and the highest heels you've got to show off those amazing legs."

I quickly end the call and mentally calculate everything I can accomplish in that time span.

"Ms. Vargas, do you have your report ready?"

My head jerks up at the unexpected question, and I spot the person looming in the doorway. "Yes, Dr. Johnson. I'm just printing it now."

"Sounds to me like you were making plans to go out tonight."

"It's my best friend's birthday. The report was emailed to you and the rest of the team about a half hour ago. I'm printing my report now, and our assistant will have it bound so you have hard copies for you to give to the investors."

"Ms. Vargas, the investors will be here next week. You'll need to be prepared to speak with them."

"Of course, Dr. Johnson. I have my teaching partner prepared to cover my lectures, and once you know the day and time, I'll be here."

"If we don't get this funding, then you can kiss your PhD goodbye."

"I understand, sir. I'll be here on Monday morning nice and early." I pack up my things for the night. I have a few more things I can do after I do my obligatory drink with Ellie.

"Have a good night," I say as I wave to the receptionist and walk out the door.

I know when this is all over and I'm awarded my PhD, this will all be worth it. I'm tired of working underneath grouchy curmudgeons like Dr. Vance Johnson. Just because his technique was awarded a Lasker Award for his approach on how to introduce new medications to the brain doesn't mean he can treat me like shit. I believe in this project with or without him. If we don't get this funding, I will do whatever it takes to get it on my own.

When I walk in the door of my studio apartment, all I want to do is crawl into my bed. Hiding under the covers and sleeping for a few hours sounds so appealing, but I have papers to grade and more research data to go through if I'm going to go out with Ellie tonight.

Sitting down, I pour myself a glass of white wine and start grading. Sometimes drinking is the only thing that keeps me from losing my cool with these students. I'll never understand how some of them got into as prestigious of a university as Berkeley, and others seem to be just pissing it all away. When I get through the papers, I glance at the time. Ellie will be here in a little more than a half hour.

I heat up the curling iron and put some spiral curls in my long dark hair and make a smoky eye and add a deep red lipstick to go with my little black dress and high-heeled shoes. They have a red sole, but I'm fairly certain that the street vendor I bought them from isn't a licensed vendor of expensive come-hither shoes, but I love them nonetheless.

I'm just finishing when I hear the horn sound outside the apartment, and my cell phone pings my friend's arrival. I grab the small gift from the table and head out the door. I'm going to have fun tonight.

chapter

TWO

CHRISTOPHER

Lying back and watching *SportsCenter* with my buddy Ryan from undergrad, we're drinking beers and debating the important things in life.

"I think the Cubs may just do it again this year," I say out loud probably more wishful thinking than a possibility.

"From your lips to God's ears, man."

"How did your job interview go today?"

"It went okay," Ryan shares. "I think they'll offer me the job, but I may want more equity than they are willing to give me."

"I guess you'll just have to determine how bad you want to move out to the coast and give up those Chicago winters."

"I know I'm ready for some warmer weather, but I have a good gig at Merck."

"You don't have any equity at Merck, so it wouldn't be much of a difference," I stress.

"But Merck is established. Coming to work at a start-up could mean that I spend years at a no-name company and then, in the end, have nothing."

"Man, I told you, my company funded that start-up. If they fuck up and go under, it isn't because they have a bad idea. They just have bad management. And let me assure you, we don't like to lose money, so we will swoop in if we need to save a company from their management."

"Why can't you get them to give me equity?" he says with a slight whine in his voice.

"Not my client company, and you've got to do this on your own. I have enough to worry about with my own job."

"What could have you stressing out? You have a sweet deal. You'll clear a great salary, and you live in a city where the number of females far outnumbers the straight men. You're golden."

He's naïve to think that I can just sit back and enjoy my salary and not perform. You are only as good as your last deal, so there's a lot of pressure. "I don't know about golden. I have a good job, but all I have to do is have a bad investment, and I'm out of a job, and yes, there are a lot of hot chicks in San Francisco, but sometimes they're too much work."

"I hear ya, man."

An alert on Ryan's phone interrupts our conversation. He stares at it for a moment and then looks up at me. "I just got a text from that girl we met at lunch today. She says she and a bunch of her friends are heading to a club called The Church. Do you know it?"

"I think it's the new one in the Tenderloin."

"Is that close?"

"It's a neighborhood not too far away. We can take a rideshare over if you want to meet up with her. I can give you a key if you decide you want to stay longer than I do."

He focuses on his phone for a second and then says, "She and her friends will meet us around ten."

Looking at the clock, I see it's after nine. "Guess I should get dressed then." I head to my room to look through my closet.

Ryan was a good buddy when we were undergrads, and I wouldn't have gotten through my stats class without him, but he's not found his niche, and I'm not sure if working for one of SHN's investments is going to be his answer. When he called and asked what I knew about Caring Technologies, I was floored.

SHN invested in Caring last year before I joined the company. It's a pet project of Cynthia's. I told Ryan what little I knew and stressed that it would hurt him more than help him if he told them he knew someone at SHN. I work in biotechnologies, and my job is to talk new pharmaceutical and biotech companies into allowing us to invest in them. While it may seem counterintuitive to need to talk a start-up into taking money, there is a lot of competition for the companies that we believe have a good product. And, while SHN may have one of the biggest success rates, we also take a little more equity for our money, and we provide help from our operations team with things such as recruiting, accounting, and other areas that can distract them from what they're looking to create. Our attitude is for them to concentrate on what they do best.

• • •

The company is ten years old, and I'm the newest business development analyst and partner. I'm looking for some strong biotech companies for us to invest in. My goal is to get a few up-and-coming drug companies. It's the low-hanging fruit in the biotech world. The cost of research and development is so high for large companies that it's created a market of start-ups. These small companies are more nimble and able to create winners. They may be more expensive since they buy them after they have some proof they'll work, but they also don't have to invest in concepts that fail. The right company is extremely profitable. It's why I got into venture capital. It's a form of legalized gambling, really.

Putting on a pair of nice dark black jeans, an expensive light blue houndstooth dress shirt, and my brown Cole Haan Chukka boots and matching belt, I add a bit of gel to my unruly curls, and I'm ready to go.

"You got protection?" Ryan holds up a half dozen condoms and wiggles his eyebrows at me.

Internally, I roll my eyes. "I'm good. You think you'll need all of those?"

"Hell, yeah! She's into me." He stuffs them in his pocket.

"You don't think that giant bulge in your pocket might say you're a little anxious."

"You're probably right. Here, take two, and then if I need them, I'll get them from you."

"Whatever, man. I'd be shocked if you used even one of them."

Grabbing a rideshare, we head over to The Church. The girls have left our name on the list, so we bypass the line. The girls already have a table, and I take a chair in the corner, where I can watch the patrons dance, drink, and have fun. Ryan doesn't need a wingman, so I sit back while he and this girl chat. Her friends are cute and friendly, and one leans over and introduces herself.

"Hi. I'm Jennifer."

Jennifer is a petite redhead. She's a little bubblier than I like usually, but I'm not rude. "Nice to meet you. I'm Christopher."

"What do you do, Chris?"

This is my least favorite question, and I'm highly annoyed that she truncated my name. I'm done. That's three strikes in my book, but I'll still be polite. "I work in finance. What about you?"

"I'm a lawyer."

"Wow." I like that she's smart. "Who do you work for?"

"I just graduated, and I'm still looking. What about you?"

"Sullivan Healy Newhouse. Where did you graduate from?"

"I put myself through law school online while working. You want to dance?"

"I'm good." I need to escape, but I also don't want to screw it up for my buddy. I should play nice with this girl. "Can I get you a drink?"

"I'm good." And that's the end of that. I'm grateful she didn't recognize the name of my firm. Usually, women will try to latch on to me once they find out who I work for, but most people know it as SHN. We are the most successful venture capital fund in the Bay Area, and recently we've had some publicity that makes us more popular than we'd like.

I turn my attention back to people watching as I drink my scotch. People grind against one another in their mating dances as the drinks flow freely. Then I spot her. She's tall with dark brown hair, big brown eyes, and legs that seem to go on forever. Her dress leaves little to the imagination, and I can tell she's perfect in every way.

I don't approach her. I just watch. She seems to be celebrating something with a group of girlfriends. Paying close attention, I notice she's drinking white wine and isn't wearing a ring on her left hand.

When she and her girlfriends head to the dance floor, I notice I'm not the only man enthralled. They're attracting a lot of male attention.

chapter

THREE

ISABELLA

"What do you want to drink?" the birthday girl asks.

"Just a glass of white wine."

"What? You need to let loose, girl. How about a cosmo or a whiskey? Not a glass of watered-down wine," my best friend Ellie yells over the pulsating music.

"What are you going to drink?"

"I'm going to start with a shot of tequila and then have a paloma."

"Isn't that tequila and grapefruit soda?"

She nods and grins widely.

"I'll get it," I offer.

Ellie heads to the reserved table with her other friends while I squeeze myself up to the bar, where I find the bartender is very attentive—my cleavage helps. He checks me out while drying his hands on a towel attached to his waist. "What can I get the beautiful lady?"

I order our drinks, and while the bartender prepares them, I scope out the place. I spot a strange guy watching me. It's a little unnerving, so I don't make eye contact or smile, and yet he decides to approach me anyway. As he sidles up to the bar next to me, my stomach clenches and my heart beats faster but not in an excited way.

"Hello. You're very beautiful." His cheap cologne is overpowering as he invades my personal space. It's creepy.

"Thank you." I turn away and pay for the drinks the bartender has placed in front of me.

"I'll get your drinks," Creepy Guy offers.

I paint a tight smile on my mouth and say, "Thank you, but my boyfriend would probably be upset if you did that." The bartender gives me a knowing look as he takes my money. "Keep the change," I tell him and gather my drinks. It's a more generous tip than I would normally give, but I need to get away from this guy.

"What can I get you?" the bartender asks Creepy Guy, trying to distract him so I can get away.

Ignoring the bartender, he leans in and growls in my ear, "Your boyfriend never has to know."

"But I'd know." I try to walk away, but he steps in front of me, blocking my getaway. "Please move," I say, but I don't wait for him to comply. Instead, I sidestep and push past him, nearly spilling my drink.

"You're a cock tease," he yells as I walk away.

I'm startled by his aggressiveness, and an automatic apology falls from my lips. "I'm sorry. I didn't mean to lead you on." I leave quickly, knowing I've dodged a bullet with the psycho.

When I reach the table, I hand Ellie her drinks and inform her, "You owe me."

"Was that weird guy hitting on you?"

I'm not going to ruin her night by sharing what an ass he was, so I roll my eyes, letting her know she was right. "Just ignore it. We're here to celebrate your birthday."

We all lift our glasses in a toast to Ellie. She slams her shot and announces, "Let's dance." There is no arguing with the birthday girl, so we make our way to the dance floor as a group. It's not long before some of the girls begin to break off to dance with men, but I stick with Ellie, content to have fun with my friend.

It's crowded on the dance floor, so I don't think twice when a hand grazes my ass. But then a set of hands wrap around me, and a body presses against me from behind, dancing with me. I jerk away and turn to discover it's Creepy Guy. I move to the other side of our group to get away, but he follows me. By this point, Ellie has started dancing with someone else, so she doesn't notice that Creepy Guy is a little too close for comfort.

He leans in, and I can smell his putrid breath. "Do you want to get out of here?"

"Thanks, but I've already told you, I have a boyfriend, and I'm here with my friends."

I stop dancing and make a beeline for the bar. I catch Ellie's eye as I pass. She glances between me and Creepy Guy before nodding in understanding. I'm retreating to the bartender, so I can ask for a bouncer if I need help.

I order a club soda. Creepy Guy sidles up to me and puts his hand on my ass. "You're so beautiful. Why did you leave me on the dance floor? We were made for each other."

I've been nice, and I've ignored him, but he isn't getting it. I need to be firm and direct. "You need to leave me alone."

chapter

FOUR

CHRISTOPHER

I watch a man approach her on the dance floor. By his rigid, mechanical movements, short hair, and buff build, I'd bet he's been in the military. When he grinds against her, she jerks away and dances to the other side of the group, but he follows her. Looking annoyed, she stalks off the dance floor and heads to the bar just down from me.

As she flags down the bartender, the man slides up next to her and grabs her ass. Okay, I've had enough of this guy, and he doesn't seem to be getting the hint. I find myself standing next to her just as she pushes him away.

"Sweetheart! There you are."

She looks at me confused. Instinct overcomes reason, and I slide an arm around her shoulder and pull her close to my side before I think better of it. Her body stiffens for just a moment, but then she relaxes and turns into my chest. My heart squeezes even tighter. Kissing her on the forehead, I look over at the guy who's been harassing her.

"Are you bothering my fiancée?"

He holds his hands up. "She didn't tell me she was engaged when she was all over me on the dance floor."

I reach for her hand, and she holds on tightly. "Well pal, move along and leave her alone."

As he walks away sulking, she leans in and says, "Thank you. He wasn't taking the hint."

"I saw that. He's still watching us. I'm afraid if you want to lose this guy, we're going to have to play this up, at least until he loses interest and moves on to someone else."

She smiles at me. "I guess that wouldn't be so bad. What's your name?"

"Christopher. And yours?"

"Bella."

"Great to meet you, Bella. What brings you to The Church?"

"It's my best friend's twenty-eighth birthday."

"She must be your much older friend then."

"You are quite the charmer, aren't you?" She gives me a brilliant smile, and I see two adorable dimples. I have the rogue thought that I could stare at her forever. Then our eyes meet, and I'm sure the world stops spinning. Everything else falls away until we are the only two people left on the planet.

"I try. Should we dance or do something to get this guy to move on?" I ask not ready to part company. I suddenly want to get to know everything about her.

She looks at her watch. "I guess we should. I need to be home around midnight."

"Why? Do you turn into a pumpkin?"

"No. I just have a busy week ahead."

• • •

We weave our way through the crowd of dancing people to the middle of the dance floor under the mirrored disco ball. My skin tingles beneath the thin fabric of my shirt as her hand slides across my chest. The casual touch sends a jolt of electricity through my entire body, spurring all kinds of thoughts, none of them pure. I want her hands on my skin, her lips pressing against mine, her body below, above, against me any way she wants, as many times as she wants.

The music shifts to a song with a softer beat, and I turn her around pressing her back against my chest as I dance with her from behind. She lays her head back on my shoulder, and our fingers thread together under her breasts as she works her ass over my dick, making it hard as a steel pole. Her dark hair is settled over her left shoulder, giving me perfect access to the right side of her neck. She smells like honey, lavender, and a hint of cinnamon.

She turns her head and stares up into my eyes. "You're very handsome."

"Thank you. You're absolutely beautiful."

My hands slide to her hips as we sway together to the music, but then her hands cover mine, and she moves them up to her breasts. They are magnificent, round and soft, and her nipples pebble beneath my touch. She wants me as bad as I want her.

She flirts mercilessly with me. Our dancing has become foreplay of what we both know is to come. This woman has my number, and I believe I have hers. I lick around the shell of her ear and shove my cock up against her ass. "You're delaying the inevitable."

"Mm, patience."

I can't help myself, and I dive right in, claiming her mouth, taking what's mine for tonight. She tastes like a fine wine. She turns to me, and our bodies fit together perfectly as we sway as one on the dance floor.

• • •

Her kiss is as sweet as I imagined as her tongue moves with mine. Tasting. Teasing. Licking. Exploring. There's a give and take. We push and pull, fighting for control.

Fuck, she's sexy. I like a woman who's not afraid to go after what she wants. She turns back around, pressing against my dick again. The thought of pulling out my cock and fucking her right here in the middle of the dance floor crosses my mind. Everyone else is in their own little worlds, doing the same thing we are. Nobody would know.

I rub my thumb over one of her nipples hidden beneath her dress and thin bra, and she gasps. My cock aches. Just knowing I can touch her and make her sound so breathless and needy is a major turn on. "Bella," I growl in her ear. I can't wait to hear her crying out my name. Soon. My hand glides down the swell of her breast and along her ribs, loving the feel of her curves as I grip her hips. I have to bite back all the pent-up sexual frustration.

Fuck, I want to bend her over and spank her for doing this to me, making me want her this bad. The only thing stopping me is the scandal it'd bring to the firm when I get charged with indecent exposure and lewd conduct.

I have a feeling Bella's pussy would be worth the risk. But I've worked too damn hard to build my career to throw it all away for something that's already guaranteed. I work my way to the top of her thigh, my fingers inching up under the hem of her dress. I'm dangerously close to her pussy.

"Oh, God," she whimpers when I tug her dress up another half an inch.

"Look at you, such a naughty little girl," I murmur in her ear as she grinds her hips in an attempt to get closer to my fingers.

"God, don't stop talking. Touch me."

Fuck, I love my life. "I love how dirty you are. You want me to fuck this little cunt with my fingers, right out here in front of everyone, don't you?"

She gasps when I slide my hand up her dress and cup her pussy. We are concealed by all the people around us. We aren't paying attention to them, and they aren't paying attention to us. Fuck, she's soaked through her panties for me. I slide her panties to the side and glide my finger back and forth through her slick folds.

A weird feeling at the back of my neck has me looking up, and I see our creepy friend watching us from the balcony of the VIP area. He raises his glass to me. Asshole. But I'm knuckle-deep in Bella's hot pussy, so a head nod will have to suffice. I remove my finger and spin Bella around. When she looks at me, I shove my pussy-soaked finger in her mouth. Her eyes widen, and I lean in next to her ear. My finger is still in her mouth, her tongue working around it.

"That's what my cock's going to taste like in an hour." A tremble courses through her body. I pull my fingers from her mouth, and she sucks them clean as if she doesn't want to let go. Her arms hook around my neck, and our mouths connect once more. Her tongue is needy and tastes like champagne.

"We're leaving, now."

"God, you're bossy."

"Well, I'm the goddamn boss."

"Hey." She grabs me by the arm and gives me a look that says be serious for a minute. "I don't normally do… this." Her eyes dart around. "I don't sleep with men on the first date."

"Good thing it's not a date."

That gives her pause, and her lips quirk into a smile. "I need to let my friends know I'm leaving."

"Of course."

I walk her to her friends but give her a moment alone with them. I wave to my friend, but he's occupied. He has a key. When she comes back to me, I haul her toward the door. I make sure to shoot that asshole the fucking bird when Bella looks the other direction. Cocksucker. A rideshare's already parked up front and waiting.

I don't feel the slightest bit of guilt for leaving Ryan. Even if I didn't like Bella, I wouldn't share. No fucking way. Bella is mine. She belongs to me. For the night… and maybe more than that, if I want more.

chapter

FIVE

ISABELLA

I've never had a one-night stand, but Christopher's the perfect candidate to start with. I've always played it safe, made sure I was in a relationship and commitments were made before falling into bed with someone. Maybe it's time to do things differently. No attachments. No broken hearts or hurt feelings.

Who needs to be tied down in a large city like San Francisco? I can sleep with him, and then we can part ways. What are the chances I'll ever see him again? Maybe Ellie is right about fate and all that shit. All I know is the chemistry between us is sizzling hot, and I need to get laid. Nature has provided me with an opportunity, so fuck it.

• • •

My heart pounds hard. The blood in my veins turns to a roar in my ears. I reach for him, drinking him in like I've been lost in the desert without water.

I have no idea where I am. We made out in the car all the way to his place. Normally, I'd be embarrassed to make out with a virtual stranger, but for some reason, it doesn't bother me tonight. Maybe it's the alcohol. Maybe it's the undeniable chemistry. Or maybe it's just the new me.

As he pulls me into an apartment, I catch that it's large and beautifully furnished. Then he draws me to him, and I only see him. We devour one another as he moves us to his bedroom. He pushes me back on the bed, and my heart races as Christopher slowly lifts his shirt over his head, tousling his hair. My breath catches as I see his rippled chest in the flesh. His physique is beautiful beyond my imagination. It's clear he works out hard. I can't take my eyes off his six-pack. His skin's so smooth and tan. It's everything I fantasize about and more. My hands tingle with a desperate need to feel his skin. My eyes travel down the thin happy trail that leads into his pants before my gaze scrolls up again and lands on the tattoo on the left side of his torso. There is a world with the words *"You must be the change you wish to see in the world." – Gandhi.* I trace my fingers over the quote and the earth.

His hands tangle in my hair as he pulls my mouth toward his. Those tempting lips crush over mine. His tongue, rough and hot, dips into my mouth when I open. I reach for him before I even realize what I'm doing, grasping his arms at the elbows. Dark flashes of arousal course through me, erupting in my center, spreading through every limb and nerve ending.

He tastes like whiskey, smells like cedarwood and a hint of clove, and feels like pure heaven.

I unbuckle his pants, and they fall to the floor. His cock escapes his boxers, and I wrap my hand around his hardness and slowly stroke him. I can't help but moan. It's perfect in every way. One look and I shudder with excitement.

He rips at my dress and buttons go flying. "Sorry," he says, but I don't care. I'm on fire, and I need him to cool me off. I drop my dress with his in a pool on the floor. I need him. "You make me so hot," he says as his fingers explore my opening. I lift my leg up to give him easier access. I'm already dripping. He presses two fingers in me, fucking me fast as he slides them in and out.

I stroke his hard cock in unison. All I can think about is how I want to fuck him until I can't see straight. His thumb finds my hard nub, and my clit throbs as he presses against it, adding just the right amount of pressure. My back arches in pleasure. "Ohmigod," I groan against him.

He presses harder and adds a third finger, causing my fingers to grip his arm. It's been so long since anything has invaded my channel. My pussy is nice and tight, and he seems to love how much I grind against his hand, showing how much I enjoy every second he's inside me. But I need more. Pulling his hand from my wetness, he unsnaps my bra so my tits fall out.

"You're so fucking perfect, with your nipples hard and aroused."

He devours my breasts, licking and suckling my nipples, before pausing to pull a condom from the bedside table. His cock ready, I wrap my legs around him and watch as he eases me onto his massive thickness. I gasp as he slowly fills me. It's tight, but it's glorious. He moves ever so slowly until I fully accommodate him, and in my anxiousness, I bounce my pussy against his perfect fucking cock. I'm not taking this slow. No. Slow is for love. This is a one-night stand, and we're doing it fast and hard.

I'm not sure when we fell asleep last night. I didn't mean to spend the night. As I look over my shoulder, I see him sleeping peacefully in his bed with the sheets wrapped around his torso. Just the sight of him turns me on. I could go for another round, but I need to get a few things done.

I don't feel too bad about slipping out this morning. Rain drizzles outside the window, casting an eerie gray light through the room, and I'm afraid if I stay, it will either be awkward and I'll wish I'd left, or we'll be repeating last night for the rest of the weekend, and I have too much to get done. I call a rideshare. Thank goodness for GPS because I'm not 100 percent sure I know where I am—I'm pretty sure I'm somewhere in Pacific Heights.

It was incredibly enjoyable, and boy did I need the exercise, but it was a one-night stand. I think about how much fun we had together. I've never experienced anything like this. Holy shit was he amazing, and I can't help but worry that he may have wrecked me for all others.

When I get home, I look at my watch and see it's not too early to call Ellie. I should check in with her to make sure she got home last night. The phone rings, and a sleepy Ellie answers. "Hullllo?"

"Hey. Are you alone?"

"What happened last night?"

"You mean the four shots of tequila you had or that creepy guy?"

She moans into the phone. "Don't say the word tequila to me for a long time."

"So, I guess that means you feel like shit." I laugh. I knew when she was starting with shots it was going to be a rough day today.

"Shh… not quite so loud. Did you go home with that hot guy last night?"

"Maybe." I bite the corner of my lip as I think about the look on his face each time he came. I shiver with excitement just imagining it, and I want to burn it into my memory.

"You never go home with anyone."

"I can't explain it, but his touch was magnetic, and I've never experienced chemistry like that with anyone."

"When are you going to see him again?"

"Never. I left before he got up this morning." This may be my biggest regret in life, but the timing right now isn't right.

"What? Why?"

Taking a deep breath and letting it out slowly, I tell her, "Because it was a one-night stand. It was never meant to be anything else. I can't manage a guy with everything else going on right now."

"But having regular amazing sex would be a bonus to your crazy schedule."

She's right, but I know that there is no such thing as just sex for me. "We didn't exchange anything other than our first names."

"You know where he lives."

"In a zip code well above my budget."

"He's rich too?" If I let her get too into this, she'll be convinced he's some Prince Charming, and she'll forget I have no way to get ahold of him.

"Maybe. You never know. Some people spend money they don't have. But he had nice stuff and a kitchen to die for."

"Listen to you. Are you going to hang out at The Church in hopes of meeting him again?"

"Nope. I have a full day of work today. I need to finish grading the papers I didn't get to last night, write a quiz for my undergrads for Monday, and finalize the proposal for another potential investor." I change the subject so she doesn't get too caught up in my stuff. "How did it go last night for you?"

"I danced with a few guys. No one really stands out to me. Marianne made sure I got home."

I cringe. I adore Marianne, and I'm grateful she was there, but I fell down on my one job last night. "Sorry about that. I wasn't a very good best friend last night."

"I'm glad you found someone to break your celibacy streak."

"It wasn't a record." Well, it might be, but I'm not going to admit to how long it's been since I've been naked with anyone.

Her voice softens. "Thanks for coming out with me last night and making my birthday special."

"I had fun, and it sounds like you did too."

"Let's go out to celebrate over lunch next Saturday—just the two of us."

"Sounds perfect. Love you!"

"Love you too."

I glare at my computer screen, the blinking cursor only accentuating the tension headache behind my eyes. I have so much to do, so I've come in to work super early to make sure I can answer any questions. I'm not sure when the investor is coming, and I don't want to ask and give Dr. Johnson another reason to gripe at me.

"Ms. Vargas, we're here to work, not to daydream," Dr. Johnson grumbles, bringing me out of my thoughts.

"Sorry." I give him a lame excuse. "I was going through some possible alternative therapies to regenerate brain cells we may not have thought of."

"Ms. Vargas, that isn't why you are here. Stick to your job."

Asshole. "Yes, sir."

I roll my eyes internally and concentrate. This company was my idea, driven by my dissertation. I regularly regret that I contacted Dr. Johnson to help because of his name and his procedure on drug delivery. But if I can help to find a cure for Parkinson's, in the end, that is all that will matter. Glancing at the clock on my computer screen, I see it's already after eight and I've been here for four hours. I have an hour to get over to Berkeley and be ready for my nine o'clock class.

I begin to pack up.

"Ms. Vargas, where are you going?"

"It's Monday. I teach Monday mornings. I will review the latest data that the techs are pulling and put it together for you and the potential investors this evening and have it for you tomorrow. When is the prospective investor coming in? I'll need a little bit of notice so I can get my class covered. Do you want to make time to go over the information tomorrow? I can be here at your convenience."

He lets out an exasperated sigh and mutters, "This is not acceptable. I don't know why you're wasting your time. You are not focused enough to pull this over the finish line."

"Dr. Johnson, that isn't true. I'm doing my required work for my studies, and I'm giving this company, which I founded, more than fifty hours a week."

"Yes, that 'founded' thing. We may have to revisit that."

My heart beats faster. There is no way he is going to snake this company out from under me. No fucking way. "There is nothing to discuss. We have a contract. If you want out, we can discuss that. But I have to leave, or I'll be late for my class." With that, I finish packing up my things and head out the door.

I don't trust the man. He's made a few comments that put me on edge. I came to him with the idea, and if the investor thinks he can work around me, or take me out, then I'll go apeshit all over them. No. This is my idea.

• • •

I realize I'm gripping the steering wheel so tightly my fingers begin to cramp. Shaking them out, I take a few deep breaths and try to not let him get to me. We hired a good attorney to draft our agreement.

Drudging along in the slow traffic on the Bay Bridge and crossing into the East Bay before heading north into Berkeley does nothing for my stress levels. I circle the parking garage and can't find a parking space. Why does this happen when I need to be on time? This is ridiculous. I finally pull into a spot between two large trash dumpsters. It's most likely not a legal spot. I'm going to roll the dice and hope that I don't get a ticket.

I race into class just on time. "Good morning, everyone. Over the weekend you were supposed to review chapters twenty-three through thirty-five."

Two-hour lectures always wipe me out. So after spending a good thirty minutes following class talking to my anxious students, I wander back to my car. There's an empty space where I left it. It isn't there. Shit. No one would steal a ten-year-old Honda Civic.

I look up at the ceiling in the parking garage and spot a partially covered sign behind the lid of one of the dumpsters saying it's a tow-away zone. I fight back the tears and anxiety that creep over me. I have an enormous amount of data to go through, a dozen emails from students to answer, and I need to find my fucking car. I'm mad at myself, and I'm blaming Dr. Johnson. He got me so upset I didn't see the stupid tow-away zone sign. Damn.

Pulling out my cell phone, I see the battery is at one bar. Can this day get any worse? Why is it that I can't get everything going right in the same direction? I call the tow company listed on the sign.

"Ah, you're the Honda Civic?"

"Yes." I breathe in and out of my nose, trying to calm myself.

"Well, your car's been sent to our lot in Walnut Creek."

"Walnut Creek?" That's two hours in the opposite direction of where I live.

"That's right. Your plates are expired, so it went into our impound lot. The cost is $2,300 cash to get your car out."

"First, my plates don't expire until the end of the month. Second, the stickers are in the glove box. Third, my car isn't even worth $2,300." I disconnect the call. I'm so angry I can't see straight.

"Professor Vargas?"

I turn and try to put a smile on my face. "Hi, Melanie. How are you?"

"I think I may be doing better than you."

"Probably. My car was towed. My fault. I was running behind and parked it here."

"Do you need a ride somewhere? I'm happy to help."

"That's very nice of you. I think they can keep the car at this point."

"Really?"

"Yep. I'll probably come to my senses in a few days, but I've got too much to do to worry about it now. Thank you for the ride offer. I'm going to go work in the Main Library, and I'll take a rideshare or BART back into the City."

"Okay. Do you want my number in case you change your mind?"

"That's very sweet of you, Melanie. I'll be okay."

She turns and leaves, and I glare one more time at the partially hidden sign. Hitching my backpack onto my shoulder, I hike across campus. In the Main Library, I find a quiet table and log on to the school Wi-Fi and begin the compilation of my evaluation. If nothing else, I can't let Dr. Vance Johnson have a reason to take my idea from me.

• • •

When my stomach growls, begging for sustenance, I look at the clock. It's after nine. I haven't eaten since this morning, and I'm starved. I pull a granola bar from my bag and munch on it. Now that I need to pay to get back into San Francisco, I can't waste any money, and I have food in my fridge at home. I set the alarm on my phone to remind me to not miss the last train back into town, and then I get back to work.

The last train is at midnight. It'll take me an hour to get into San Francisco, and then I'll need a ride to my apartment. If I leave the Main Library by eleven-thirty, I'll make the last train. Now that I have a plan, I can concentrate on my students' emails, analyze all the data, and keep myself from getting too far behind.

My alarm goes off, but I snooze it twice squeezing out as much time as I can. I just barely make the platform and find a spot on the crowded train. Most of the people are drunk, and it's another lesson in patience. I fight the sleep on the train which ends up being easier as I eavesdrop on the drunk conversation going on behind me. They're debating what is the best peanut butter brand. Their back-and-forth is really entertaining, and I come close to telling them that it's Jif Peanut Butter, but instead I listen and laugh. When I arrive at Union Station, I exit and see the large group of people waiting at the bus stop and decide, rather than take MUNI across town to my place, I'll call up a rideshare.

It's 1:30 a.m. by the time I walk into my apartment. I head straight to the kitchen and open a can of vegetable soup. While it heats, I do several squats and a few jumping jacks to get my blood pumping to fight fatigue and sleep. I have a lot to get accomplished and still a few hours of work to get through before I have to be at the lab.

When I finally enter the last bit of information into the proposal, I look at the clock and see that it's after four. I can sleep for three hours. My body relaxes knowing that sleep is imminent. Three hours of sleep isn't perfect or nearly enough, but at least it's something. I don't even take the time to change. I just crawl into bed and throw my covers over me. I think I'm asleep before my head even hits the pillow.

When the alarm goes off just a short while later, I feel more tired than I was before the nap, and I have another long day ahead of me. I give myself a pep-talk and remind myself, I can do this. There is a light at the end of the tunnel, and I can always sleep later.

chapter
SIX

CHRISTOPHER

It's been three days since I fucked Bella, and I can't get the memory of her pussy out of my mind. I've picked up the phone several times, tempted to reach out to her, but then I remember I don't have her information. She left before we could exchange it. I'm mad at myself for not thinking rationally and getting her digits. It's ridiculous.

I've not had that much sex in a long time. I can't believe I brought her back to my place. I never bring women home. Usually, I'll grab a room and leave after I'm done. With Bella, it seemed natural to bring her back to my condo.

When I woke that morning, I was sporting my morning wood and ready to take her again, but when I reached for her, the bed was cool to the touch. I rolled over, and she had gone. No note. Nothing.

I'm more than disappointed. It's usually me who runs out. I can't decide if I'm mad because she left me without saying goodbye, or if it was because I didn't get to kick her out—which I never would have done, but she made the decision to leave without consulting me.

Normally, after I fuck a woman so hard, she can barely walk, and I can't get away from her fast enough. *Why is she different?*

The challenge. It's been a while since I've had one.

Growing more irritated with every passing second, I know I'm not rational. I toss my cell phone in the top drawer of my desk and bury myself in work.

Cynthia peeks into my office. "Hey, you up for joining Mason, Dillon, and me for lunch today?"

"Sure. What's the occasion?"

"We'll be talking about what's in our pipelines for budgeting purposes."

My stomach drops. The saying in this business is that "You're only as good as your last deal," and I haven't had one in a while. Cynthia recently had two big wins. I look over what I have going on, and I grow uneasy. We had a deal go sideways with a hacker, and our plans for investing may become curtailed.

"What time?"

She studies me for a moment. "You have nothing to worry about. I asked for the meeting given recent events with Pineapple Technologies and wanted to see how much rope we have to dangle. I'm including William too."

A small bit of relief crawls through me. I nod. "Great. I'm good with joining you."

"Perfect. Let's try for twelve thirty in the lobby. I'll work on a lunch reservation."

"See you in a few then."

I pull a few things together and line up a few files so I'm prepared for lunch.

• • •

I walk to the lobby with my leather portfolio and some notes on my pipeline of prospective ventures. The list of possible investments could wrap around San Francisco multiple times, but our goal at SHN is to be a sole investor. We don't have deep experience in biotech since we just started concentrating on it when I joined, so it's been a bigger challenge for us to break into than any of us expected. I've had some minor wins, but I'd feel more secure with a bigger win. I'm still presented with more opportunities than we could ever fund, and those that really pop have most of our competitors chasing them.

I'm first to arrive in the lobby. Emerson stops by. She oversees the firm's operations and is married to Dillon, another partner. "Hey, I hear you all are headed to Wetbar for lunch. Very nice."

Good to know. Nice restaurant. "Should be good."

"I interviewed someone recently who would make a good person on-site, so I'm hoping you and Cynthia have something coming up so I can hire him."

Cynthia has walked up during our discussion and joins in. "I hope so too. With Pineapple Technologies tanking after the hackers went to town on them, and our recent investments in two other start-ups, DribbleDrabble and Care, I know we're both getting some great ideas come across our desks, But I don't want to overextend us."

Emerson nods. "I appreciate that. Dillon can be tough to live with when he's too stressed. His golf game goes in the tank, and it gets too hard to let him win."

"You never let me win," Dillon says as he and Mason arrive. Looking carefully at Cynthia and me, he shares, "She could beat any woman on tour, and many of the men, and is entirely too competitive to let anyone beat her."

"Just trying to share your manliness." She winks at him and waves as we enter the elevator.

"Don't worry, I think you're manly," Mason says with a grin.

"I think it's totally hot that she can beat the socks off of me. I can run numbers much faster than she can," Dillon explains.

"There, there, Dillon. I think you're manly too," Cynthia insists.

Everyone looks at me. "Okay, I think you're manly too."

We are all laughing before we hit the lobby of our building and walk the three blocks to the restaurant.

We are seated facing the Bay Bridge and Treasure Island. Mason is the managing partner, and Dillon oversees our portfolio and, in a traditional sense, is our chief financial officer. William Bettencourt, our newest partner, has been with us a few weeks and is tasked with bringing in financial-based start-ups into our fund.

After we order lunch, Cynthia thanks everyone for coming and says, "I know with the challenges following Pineapple and recently having won two good accounts, I thought we should have a conversation about available funds. An interesting prospectus came across my desk yesterday. It's a new venture by Tisdale, but they are looking for twenty million right out of the gate. William has some things churning but is too new to have too much."

William nods.

"Christopher has two strong prospects he's working on. How much money are they looking for and what's their timeline?" she inquires.

I'm relieved that she's making sure they hear what I have going on. "I'm meeting with Black Rock Therapeutics this week, and they are looking for an initial ten million, but ultimately they will need roughly three hundred million to go to market."

Mason interjects, "That's the Parkinson's drug with a different delivery system?"

I nod. "If they can get it going, it would be very attractive for some of the bigger pharma companies to buy. Getting it to market on its own would be expensive, but it could flip early if their research is solid."

"It was founded by the Lasker Award winner, wasn't it?"

"Yes." I take out a file for another company I'm interested in. "I also like MiscCo. They are doing some aggressive research into the next generation of artificial joints."

"How much are you projecting they will want?"

"Benchmark is looking at them heavily, and they want between fifteen and twenty million with an eventual spend of two hundred million."

Dillon whistles. "Wow, that's big. Benchmark doesn't have that kind of cash. Where would they get that?"

I shrug. "I'm not sure. I know their emerging markets guy and can find out what they are looking at. We've never really comingled money with other VC firms. Is that something we would consider?"

"I think that is a good conversation for Sunday night's partner meeting," Mason answers.

"So that brings me back to why I wanted this meeting. Dillon, how much investment funds do we have and where are things going forward?" Cynthia asks.

"I think we need to discuss this as a group. I don't want to get too thin with our cash flow, but if something like Black Rock were to come in and turn quickly, that would be a big deal."

"I'll know more by Wednesday," I assure the group.

• • •

When lunch wraps up, I'm not sure we've come to any conclusions. Cynthia was hoping to get a green light to talk about how much she has when she interviews start-ups about what they're looking for. Our previous budgeting had been planned with the income we were expecting to make from Pineapple Technologies before it died, using the profit we made off of them. We're just happy we got our investment back.

Lying in bed, I think about Bella. I wonder how I can find her again. I've heard stories of people placing personal ads, but that seems a bit sleazy. I've searched for her PeopleMover page, but couldn't find her.

Why didn't you get her contact information?

I thought I'd have all the time in the world to ask her questions about where she worked and her family. I'm going to go back to The Church on Saturday night and hope to see her.

Please let her be there.

chapter
SEVEN

CHRISTOPHER

It's Wednesday morning, and I have an appointment with one of my more interesting prospects. Rather than worry about parking, I take a rideshare into the SOMA neighborhood. The company is located on a street lined with multiple warehouses, where one white building seems to blend with the next. The GPS tells the driver we've arrived, and I get out, hoping the door in front of me is the right place. The nondescript building doesn't look like much, but once inside, I find a decked-out lab.

I walk up to the receptionist and introduce myself. "Hi. I'm Christopher Reinhardt from SHN, and I'm here to meet with Dr. Vance Johnson."

She grins widely as she stands and extends her hand. "Welcome to Black Rock Therapeutics. My name is Mindy. Dr. Johnson's expecting you, and I'll let him know you've arrived."

As I wait in the reception area, I take in all the old issues of science periodicals that are scattered along the table. I don't have to wait long before he comes walking out.

Dr. Johnson is a short, round, balding man who reminds me of a weasel. It's hard to believe this man won the Lasker Award. "Mr. Reinhardt, thank you for coming in. We're excited you're here." We shake hands.

"Nice to finally meet you face-to-face."

"Would you care for a tour of our lab?"

"I'd love one."

He leads me into the lab, talking as he goes. I notice that none of the employees seem to look him in the eye as they scuttle out of his way. He takes a lot of the credit for what his team has accomplished. I would imagine he is a difficult manager. That would be a red-flag for Emerson and her team.

The tour ends at a large conference room that is set up with a huge buffet. He pulls up a PowerPoint slide presentation and walks me through the results they've accomplished so far, and it is impressive.

"The data is still pretty raw at this point, but we expect to have it ready for trials within six months."

"Animal or human?"

"Animal," he asserts firmly.

Internally I blanch. I'm not a fan of animal testing. "What are you doing to prepare for your testing?"

"I have a grad student from Berkeley's Biochemical department working on that."

"Great. Can I meet him?"

"I wish you could. Unfortunately, they're not here today. They work Tuesdays and Thursdays."

"I see. Can you tell me how you are collecting your raw data today?"

"Well, ah, as you can see, I'm using data from these Parkinson's patients and from patients who've had other brain degenerative diseases." He stumbles a bit. "It's pretty complicated."

"I see. Dr. Johnson, I've been to medical school. I think I can grasp it. Maybe I should meet with your research assistant?"

"That won't be necessary. I'd hate for you to come back again."

I leaf through the proposal and spots some changes. "I see you've upped your ask from your original proposal you sent me from ten million dollars to fifty million." That's a huge increase, and I'm not seeing why the amount would have increased so significantly.

"Yes, as we reevaluated our needs, we thought the ten million wouldn't cover all the clinical trials needed to move this forward. Animals are expensive you know."

"Dr. Johnson, this is only a preliminary trip. Let me explain how we work at SHN. Once I have a firm grasp of your concept, I will pass it along to some of the other teams. Our technology team will vet any software and prototypes. Our operations team will walk through your leadership team, your accounting, and your vendors. And a team will go through your business plan. Then together the partners will determine if you'd be a good fit for us."

"Well, I hope that doesn't take too long. I have interest from several angel investors and Perkins Klein and Carson Mills."

Perkins Klein is defunct and has been for almost a year, so I'm positive he's lying. Not a good sign. But given his anxiousness, I'll give him a pass—this time. Chances are it's his way of negotiating. It's not a good business practice, but honestly, if they are able to accomplish what they're setting out to do, this will be a huge win, and they'll have several investors lining up around the block to finance them.

"Well, if that's the case, we'll want to move quickly," I assure him, but I'm not sure he understands quickly could still mean six months.

After a two and a half-hour meeting, I'm done and ready to get out of here. I have mixed feelings on this deal. I desperately need another company in my portfolio, but I'm just not sure this is the one. The Lasker Award makes Dr. Johnson and Black Rock Therapeutics a stronger sell, but something seems a little off.

"Thank you for coming in, Mr. Reinhardt."

"Thank you for showing me around. Let me know when I can meet with your research assistant. I have a few more questions to ask that I think only he can answer."

"I'll get that set up." He smiles, but it doesn't reach his eyes. Somethings off, I just can't place it right now.

chapter

EIGHT

CHRISTOPHER

It's been a crappy weekend. I didn't accomplish anything that I wanted to get done. Instead, I spent the weekend canvassing San Francisco. I looked for Bella everywhere I could think of. Each time I saw someone with long, dark, luscious hair, my heart would beat a bit faster and my palms would sweat as I hoped it would be her, but it never was. I can't believe how disappointed that makes me.

I even went out to The Church last night to look for her. No luck. I did see that asshole there again, but he seemed to be preoccupied with another woman who was more receptive than Bella had been. Good. Now he'll fuck off.

I danced with a few girls, but it wasn't the same as it was with Bella. The chemistry that we had was different. It was more intense than I've ever experienced. I don't know how to explain it to either myself or anyone else.

Driving down the peninsula to our Sunday night meeting, William and I ride together and discuss what it's like to be the new guy at SHN. These dinners are pretty impressive. The Arnaults invite all of us over for dinner every Sunday night, and a partners' meeting follows. We can bring a guest, but they can't attend our meeting.

Margo and Charles Arnault are the original founders of Sandy Systems, which is one of the original start-ups that gave the Bay Area Silicon Valley, and they are on our advisory board, but so are their two children—Trey who currently runs Sandy Systems, and their daughter, CeCe, who runs Metro Composition, which is quickly becoming the largest independent cosmetic company in the world. Margo started Metro when she left Sandy Systems.

"Do you feel a little left out not bringing a date?" William asks me.

"Yeah, sometimes but only because I don't bring a date. It seems the dinner part is certainly social, but I've never felt left out."

"It would be nice to have that company for dinner, but who wants to come to this thing and sit around waiting for us while we sit in a meeting for two hours?"

"You're probably right, although that seems to be a pretty fun crowd. I sometimes wish I was with them rather than in the meeting," I confide.

"I hear ya, man."

When we arrive, a pack of dogs greets us, and CeCe comes out and gives us each a hug as she waves the dogs away. "Welcome to Casa Arnault."

"Nice combination of Spanish and French," I joke with her because they pronounce the Arnault name in French.

"Mucho bien." She grins widely. She's stunningly beautiful with her chestnut brown hair and a figure that is to die for, but after meeting Bella, I have eyes for no one else.

Each dinner begins with a nice mixed cocktail that Emerson has created. Tonight's drink is a honey bourbon cocktail. She hands me a glass. The dark bourbon is cloudy and over ice with an orange peel garnish. I'm prepared for a sweet drink, but I'm surprised when it's actually not sweet at all.

"This is a keeper," Sara announces. She gets lots of agreement from around the room. The honey seems to take the bite out of the bourbon.

Margo announces, "Tonight's menu is a prime rib with twice-baked potatoes and roasted brussel sprouts, and dessert will be a blueberry cobbler." I'm consistently amazed at how elaborate our meals are each week.

Sitting around the table at dinner, I look at the group and realize I really like everyone in the room, but they've all been coupling up.

Dillon and Emerson are married to one another, and I'm waiting to hear they are expecting a baby.

Sara and Trey married a while ago at some fancy wedding in Hawaii. I remember reading about it in the tabloids when I was interviewing at SHN. Trey is CeCe's twin brother and the son of Margo and Charles.

Mason brings his girlfriend, Annabelle. She's cute enough but doesn't seem to be the right fit for Mason. She seems to be a little bit of a hanger-on.

Cameron's wife, Hadlee, is a pediatrician. She grew up next door to the Arnaults, and met Cameron through CeCe. She and Cameron are huge Harley buffs and will spend their weekends riding up and down the California coast on a motorcycle all decked out in black leather outfits.

Cynthia recently got engaged to Todd. Todd is one of our new advisers. He works for a hedge fund out of New York City and moved here to start a San Francisco office when he was introduced to Cynthia by CeCe.

The only partner missing is Greer, but she and her husband are in Tuscany, Italy right now at her husband's family's quarterly wine meeting—he's one of something like fifteen kids, and they own vineyards all over the world under the family wine umbrella.

I had no idea when I joined this company that I would be joining a family, and we've all become a great group of friends.

"Christopher, so are you dating anyone?" CeCe asks suddenly. Everyone seems to stop what they are doing and listen.

"No, I've been working too hard," I tell her. "But I met a really nice girl. Unfortunately, I somehow didn't get her contact information, and I'm trying to figure out how to find her."

"Who introduced you?"

I go into the story about the asshole at the club but leave out the fact that I took her home and fucked her hard and I couldn't get enough.

"You were her knight in shining armor," Hadlee exclaims.

"Are you going back to The Church?" Margo asks.

"I went for a short time last night. She wasn't there, nor were any of her friends."

"What's her name?" CeCe enquires.

"Bella. I don't have the last name."

"I'll have to think about that one," CeCe murmurs. Turning to William, she asks, "What about you? Are you dating anyone seriously?"

"No, definitely not. I haven't found the right girl. I'm not looking at this point. I'm focused on doing a good job and making a good living."

"William and I have a friend in common, and she's over the moon about him, but…" Annabelle shares.

There's a bit of pink that creeps on his cheeks. "We went on one date and, well, never mind."

I see Annabelle is ready to continue, but Mason gives her a look. She settles for saying, "She'd love to see you again when you're ready." She then looks at Mason and shrugs.

"You know what I used to hate when I was single?" Emerson asks the group. "Being asked why I was still single, as if there is nothing better than being part of a couple."

"Well, if either of you want some help meeting the right girl, I may have some ideas for you," CeCe offers.

"You guys don't turn down CeCe's help. She has the best picker out there," Hadlee points out.

This is not how I want to decide my love life.

"Is there any more wine?" William asks, and I surmise he feels the same way.

The rest of the dinner moves to vacations people are planning. When it becomes eight o'clock, the partners and advisors retire to Charles's office, and we all take our seats in the same place as we do every single week.

Joining us first on our agenda is Jim Adelson who oversees all of our security. He walks us through some updates on what the FBI and Cameron and his team have learned about our hacker situation.

"The assistant US attorney has been successful in getting counts against Adam Ambrosia and Eve McIntosh," he shares.

"Is it a problem they don't know who Adam and Eve are?" Mason asks.

"No, it seems that they were successful in using their hacker names. They are going to hold off trying them unless we start to get close to the statute of limitations, and then they will."

"Isn't Ambrosia an apple variety?" Sara asks.

Emerson looks at her confused. "Yes."

"And McIntosh is also an apple variety?"

"Yes," Emerson says slowly.

"Well, there is a legal metaphor, the fruit of the poisonous tree. It's used to describe evidence that is obtained illegally. The logic of the terminology is that if the source—the 'tree'—of the evidence or evidence itself is tainted, then anything gained—the 'fruit'—from it is tainted as well."

Everyone stops fidgeting and processes what Sara has shared.

"The biblical reference of Adam and Eve being the first man and woman who had a poisonous apple is thought to be a description of their hubris, which expelled them from the Garden of Eden. The apple could relate to the biblical story." Looking around at all of us, she continues, "What if our hackers once saw SHN as the Garden of Eden but now see it as the poisonous tree, and the apples are our success. Since they've been expelled, they plan to chop down the poisonous tree?"

Mason sits back hard in his chair and looks between Jim and Charles, and the room erupts.

"It's just where my mind went. It is probably just two made up names, and I see something that isn't there," Sara says.

"Sara, I think that is a brilliant observation. I hadn't seen it that way. At a minimum, I think it's worth sharing with Walker Clifton in the US Attorney's Office.

"Fuuuuck," Dillon says. "Will this nightmare ever end?"

Mason sits forward with his hands on his thighs. "I agree with Jim. I think it is a brilliant observation and should be shared with the FBI cybercrimes team and the US attorney's office."

Cameron says, "I'm due to meet Cora Perry with cybercrimes later this week. I will let her know. Jim, let me know if you want to join me. I'll also see if Walker is interested in joining us too."

"Sara, how did you think of this?" Charles asks.

"Well, as I said, it's a legal metaphor that is used a lot, but also my birth parents are quite religious, and spending time with my brothers and sisters, they talk a lot about religious meanings."

• • •

"I think you may have solved a big puzzle in this case," Charles says.

We continue to talk about that for some time before we move on.

Dillon is next on the agenda. He passes out a financial statement for all of our portfolio, and it's stunning to me that there is almost a trillion dollars in value.

"As you can see, our business model is doing well for us," Dillon says.

"How are we for cash?" Cynthia asks.

"Well, we have about twenty-five million that is somewhat liquid and still have a cushion for our payroll and expenses for six months. But that is if we don't sell or take anything public. But as I understand it, we have about six transactions coming at us. Sara, is that right?"

Sara opens the portfolio notebook on her lap. "We have Page Software being sold to Moon Micro later this month."

"That should give us eighteen million," Dillon shares.

Mason stands and walks over to a whiteboard and starts to date and total what Sara and Dillon are saying.

"We then have Tsung Software at the end of the month going public, if all things line up."

Dillon looks at his notebook. "That's one of our largest sales this year, and depending on the company buying-back options, we'll be well over a hundred million in profit."

"I spoke with the bank, and they're ready once all the paperwork clears," Mason says.

"For next month, we have Fractional Technologies going public and Dream Logistics being sold." Sara closes her book and looks at Dillon.

"As long as we don't experience what happened with Pineapple Technologies," Dillon says.

"Knock on wood," William mutters.

"We should double our bottom line," Dillon confirms.

"I guess that means you need us to come up with more investments?" I tease.

• • •

"Obviously, we need to proceed with caution, but if we are able to roll the bulk of that income into new investments, that would be our goal. I know we touched on this earlier this week, but why don't each of you share what you have going on." Mason looks at William to start us off.

Opening his own notebook, he walks through four companies that sound promising. "I also have a worldwide online payments system that supports online money transfers and serves as an electronic alternative to the big gorilla that most use today." He turns to Cameron. "It seems rather revolutionary, and if you have someone from your team who can vet the software, it might be worth an investment. I think because they're in a market with someone who has the majority of the business, they will be inexpensive but, if it does what they say, will be huge."

"Not a problem. Parker is just finishing his initial phase with the FBI cybercrimes unit and may have some room on his plate. Send it over to me, and I'll get it figured out."

"Cynthia, why don't you share with everyone what you have going on," Mason nudges.

Cynthia smiles and informs us of her prospect, which seems exciting.

When it's my turn, I share what's keeping me busy. "Emerson, if you have a minute, I'd love your thoughts on something that I'm looking at."

"Of course. Let me know, and we can talk."

"Okay, guys, so when we're looking at these investments, we're looking at close to a hundred million dollars in investments. We won't invest in all of them, either by our choice or theirs, but we are in good shape."

As we break, Jim stands and gives his weekly reminder. "All right you guys, remember this information is for this room only. Try not to say anything to anyone outside of this room."

"Have a great week, everyone. I'll see you in the morning at the office," Mason concludes.

• • •

We all shuffle out of the room. "Margo, thanks again for the outstanding dinner," I tell her. These meals are better than the meals I grew up with, and they really beat the takeout I get most nights.

"You're welcome. Any special requests?"

"I have to say, I loved your meatloaf with the cheese in the middle," I share.

"That's one of my favorites too," Cynthia volunteers.

"Pasta dishes are always good," Emerson offers.

"You guys can do a pasta dish at your place any time. These dinners are supposed to be something you won't make yourselves at home," Margo admonishes her.

CeCe puts her arm around her mother's shoulder and says, "You're spoiling us."

"And she loves doing it," Charles says from behind me.

"Whatever you make will be fantastic," I add. "See you next week."

William and I make our way out the door. Once we're firmly in the car and driving toward the 101, he says, "I was surprised to see the portfolio tonight. I've seen parts of it, but not like it was tonight. I know that each of the founders are listed as billionaires in the *Silicon Valley Business Journal,* which tells me it's a possibility for both of us and quickly."

I agree. As I drop him at his place in Nob Hill, I continue on to Pacific Heights where I watch some television and relax.

Lying in bed, my mind drifts to Bella. I don't want to wash my sheets quite yet because I swear I can still smell her scent on the pillow. I really need to find her. I need to figure out a way to get to her. I don't know what magic spell she cast upon me, but I can't help but think this is the woman for me.

chapter

NINE

ISABELLA

"Another week, another dollar?" Ellie asks.

"Hard to say. I keep waiting for Dr. Johnson to tell me when we're meeting with the investors."

"I bet he can't get them to talk to him. Bella, I know why you think you need him, but I don't trust that man."

"And that is why I adore you." I give her a hug.

"Where is your car?" Ellie asks.

"You don't want to know." It's been two weeks. I'm still mad and haven't bailed it out of impound. With a big sigh and a lot of prompting, I tell her what happened.

"You mean you're without a car?"

"Public transportation in The City is fine to get around and out to Berkeley."

"Wait, there is something totally wrong with what they've done to your car."

"I don't have time to figure it out, and what they want to get it out of impound is more than the car is worth. I'm good with rideshares for now. We just need to get the funding so we can move on to the next phase."

She reaches for my arm. "I know you're worried about your dad. I get it."

My father has Parkinson's, and the drugs haven't worked. He was an amazing father when I was growing up. He never missed any of my activities, and he loved me unconditionally. Most importantly, he was a great buffer between my mom and me. She was a tiger mom before the term tiger mom existed.

"I'm worried about my dad. I may not come up with a good treatment in time for him, but maybe I can for someone else."

"When will you know about the funding?"

"We haven't met with anyone, so I guess when he tells me. Dr. Johnson wanted to control that, which is fine because it keeps him out of the research side."

I give her a hug goodbye when we arrive at the lab. "Thank you so much for the ride."

"You're good to get home tonight?"

"Yep." I hold up my cell phone because it holds the app to call a rideshare.

Waving as she drives off, I walk into the lab. Our receptionist stops me. "Good morning, Isabella. Dr. Johnson is looking for you."

Glancing at my cell phone, I note that I'm early. "No problem. Do you know where he is?"

She shakes her head. "Do you want me to call his cell phone and ask?"

"Goodness, no. I'll track him down." I smile, and my stomach churns. *What does he need now?*

I drop my bag in my office and turn my computer on, letting it go through the start-up sequence while I get a cup of coffee and go in search of Dr. Johnson.

As I am pouring my first cup of coffee and eyeing the donuts that someone has brought, Dr. Johnson comes into the break room. "Ms. Vargas, you're late."

"I am? I usually don't arrive until noon on Wednesdays."

"That's not acceptable. You should be here by eight like everyone else."

"Dr. Johnson, I have a class I teach on Wednesday mornings. It's in my contract." Rather than argue with him, I change the subject. "So when are we meeting with the investor?"

"He was here last Wednesday. I think I got him locked down."

"Why didn't you tell me you were meeting with him Wednesday? This is my company. I should've been here. You don't understand the slide deck I gave you."

He looks at me with disdain. "It isn't *your* company. You left it with me to secure the funding, and the only reason people are talking to us is because of me."

I'm seething inside. "Where did he leave it?"

"I'm just waiting for him to go through our information, and he'll probably have a check for us within a month or so."

"Really? It was that easy?"

"Ms. Vargas, it is quite the coup to have me running this company. My connections get me the funding."

I'm at a loss. If getting the money is this easy, we are in great shape. I may be able to make a difference to families like mine. "Well, great. I will begin preparing for trials."

"Yes, you do that." He turns and walks out, leaving me trying so hard to remember why I decided to ask him to join me in the venture.

I work my way back to my office the long way and check in with our staff. We're fairly small at this point with only ten employees. I greet each person and ask them how things are going with their projects and try to ask something personal since we are all working toward a common goal.

Just before I leave for a quick lunch break, Mindy rings me. "Ms. Vargas, the investor is here and would like to meet with you and Dr. Johnson, but Dr. Johnson has left to run an errand. Are you available to meet with him?"

"I'll be right up." I smooth my skirt and check my reflection in the mirror. I can do this. I walk out, and I see Dr. Johnson with his takeout lunch in his hands and see him talking to someone.

"...surprised you're here."

"I hope you don't mind. I did mention wanting to speak with your research assistant." I stop in my tracks. *Research assistant? Hell, no. What the fuck is he telling the investors?*

"Yes, well, I thought you'd make an appointment."

I appear and stop dead in my tracks. It's Christopher from the club. He looks up and recognizes me at the same moment. This can't be happening.

I extend my hand. "Hello. Welcome to Black Rock Therapeutics. I'm Isabella Vargas, co-founder and chief research officer of Black Rock."

Dr. Johnson stumbles. "Ms. Vargas, I got this. You can go back to your lab."

"Actually, I think you're the one I want to meet with," Christopher says as he shakes my hand, ignoring Dr. Johnson.

"That's not necessary. I can have you speak with Jim Thompson in our lab," Dr. Johnson insists.

I'm ready to end Dr. Johnson's contract immediately, but for the moment, I just stand there. I'm torn. I want to wring Dr. Johnson's neck, but I also want to secure the funding for this venture.

"Please, this way." I motion for Christopher to follow me. I don't know where to start. Dr. Johnson is rambling on, but I don't hear him.

Christopher speaks over him. "Dr. Johnson was kind enough to walk me through the proposal. My apologies, I didn't realize you were a co-founder. Tell me how you came up with the concept."

"That isn't really germane to the proposal," Dr. Johnson interjects.

I ignore him. "Well, I have someone close to me with Parkinson's, and as you know, Levodopa is the most effective drug to fight the disease, but the effectiveness wears off after two or three years of usage, and in some cases isn't effective at all. Our method is another drug that uses Dr. Johnson's method, for which he won the Lasker Award, to produce a new technique to get the medication to the brain. It may also have other implications for other brain degenerative diseases."

"Yes, my method makes this possible drug effective," Dr. Johnson points out.

"Are you a doctor—medical or a doctorate?" Christopher asks, ignoring Dr. Johnson.

"I'm completing my doctorate in biochemistry from Cal," I inform him.

"After she finishes her dissertation in a few years," Dr. Johnson says with disdain.

"That's true, but my course work is finished, and this project came out of my research for my dissertation."

Christopher looks at me, and I can see in his eyes he has questions that don't relate to Black Rock. We've arrived at my office. It's small, but we can fit. "I'm sorry for the cramped space, but I'd like to show you the data on my computer. I receive it raw from the lab, and I formulate the results you can see here." Both men reach for chairs in my office.

Christopher turns to Dr. Johnson "Your tour last week and presentation was outstanding, but do you think I could meet with Ms. Vargas and walk through these numbers with her? Alone."

Dr. Johnson's hands balls into fists at his side, and I've worked with him long enough to know that is a sign that he's angry. "Oh, of course." He steps out of my office, and Christopher shuts the door behind him.

I quickly write a note and show it to him, letting him know they can hear everything we say in the next office.

He nods. "So, walk me through your assumptions and data," he says with that damn sexy, lopsided grin. Caressing my hand in both of his, he reminds me what it feels like to be caressed elsewhere by those big, masculine fingers.

I spend the next forty-five minutes explaining and answering questions.

He writes a note and shows it to me, asking if we can go get coffee somewhere.

I nod.

He writes another note while I talk more about our next step in the trials we want to try.

"You aren't doing animal testing?" he asks.

"Oh goodness, no. I'm not sure we'll go that route. Right now we need to do more test-tube testing."

"That's great news." He hands me a note telling me he'll meet me beside the building in twenty minutes.

I nod again.

He stands. "Thank you, Ms. Vargas." He picks up a business card and asks, "Is this your phone and email?"

"Yes, please feel free to reach out and ask any questions you may have. I understand from Dr. Johnson that the presentation of our proposal went well, and you are encouraged."

"Well, I'm the first cog in this train. From here I pass my recommendations along to my team. A fifty-million-dollar request is pretty significant for the first round. We have operations, legal, and finance groups to sign off before we would write a check."

"Thank you for your time. We really appreciate your consideration. This project has a lot of passion behind it."

He opens the door, and I'm taken aback to see Dr. Johnson is standing there. "Can I answer any other questions for you?" he offers.

"No, I think Ms. Vargas was quite informative."

Dr. Johnson gives me a dirty look and Christopher leaves.

I sit down in my desk chair and exhale. I can't believe "my" Christopher is our possible funder. I can't be sure what Dr. Johnson told him, but it's becoming clear he didn't mention me at all.

Dr. Johnson comes marching back to my office. "How dare you meet with him without me."

"Excuse me? First, you met with him without me. And second, I didn't ask you to leave, he did." I'm so angry I'm going to say something I may regret. "I'm going to step out."

"You haven't done anything today. You can't leave."

I pick up my purse and grab my phone. "I don't know when I'll be back."

"You leave, and you can kiss your job goodbye."

I turn and look at his little weasel face. "Dr. Johnson, I think if you check the agreement we have, you will find that you can't fire me."

"I will make sure that we don't get the funding."

I walk out, leaving him talking to the door. As I exit the building, I see Christopher in a silver Mercedes SUV at the end of the building. I'm shaking mad right now, and I don't want to screw up our funding, so I use the brief moments to breathe deeply and collect myself as I walk down to him.

chapter

TEN

CHRISTOPHER

She gets into the passenger seat and smiles at me. "Well, that was quite the surprise."

Man, she has a great smile—full lips, straight white teeth. I really want to taste that mouth and feel her give in and open for me.

"I can't believe that I ran into you. I went to The Church Saturday night looking for you. Why did you leave, and why didn't you leave your number?" I ask, embarrassed I'm so open and not playing it cool at all.

"It was a one-night stand. I didn't expect you'd want to see me again."

I take a big breath. "Did you have fun?" She bites her lip and nods. My cock stands at attention, and I wish it was me biting that lip. "I did too and wouldn't mind having more fun."

"Instead of coffee, can we get lunch somewhere close?"

"Sure." I pull into a sports bar I go to when I want to watch hockey. The beers are cold, and the food is greasy. Probably not her style, but it's out of the way but close.

I park, and I hold the door for her. "This should work."

"Perfect."

It takes a moment for us to adjust our eyes from the bright light of the outside to the dim sports bar. A long wooden bar runs the length of the back walls. Huge, flat-screen TVs seem to occupy every inch of wall space. Baseball games flicker on screens, but luckily the sound is muted, so we hear only the normal rustle of any bar—glasses clinking on tables, patrons chatting, the sizzle and pop from the kitchen.

We take a seat, and I ask her, "What'll you have?"

"A diet coke but with a sandwich or something. I haven't eaten, and I have a hunger headache that's killing me."

"Lunch it is."

A waitress stops by our table, and we both order sodas and sandwiches.

A dent creases her face as her lips curl in a half smile, once again revealing her dimples in addition to the sexiest voice I've ever heard. Oh hell, I'm in trouble.

"Are you a medical doctor?" she asks.

"Yes, but I'm not licensed to practice. I went to med school and have an MBA. I always wanted to work in venture capital."

"Who grows up saying, 'I want to be a venture capitalist?' I mean, really?"

The yeah-right look she shoots me sends heat careening through my veins. I clear my throat and place my hands in my lap, so I'm not tempted to reach for her. "My father was an intellectual property attorney when he started out. I was going to follow in his footsteps, but instead used my science degree to attend medical school. Medicine bored me. The idea of dealing with the same thing over and over was a deal breaker, but I enjoyed the research side and played with that. I saw funding as an issue for most medical-related start-ups and realized that few venture capital funds understand how to invest in businesses like yours. I have a friend of a friend who introduced me to my firm, and they hired me."

"It's hard to get funding. I approached Dr. Johnson because of his notoriety after winning the Lasker Award."

Our food arrives and we dig in enjoying our lunch and not talking about work for a few moments. "This is the best ruben in all of San Francisco."

"The turkey sandwich isn't bad at all either." Her perfect mouth is devouring a hand-carved turkey, bacon, lettuce, and tomato on toasted wheat bread.

I want to know everything about her. I have thousands of questions running through my mind, but I don't want to frighten her, so I start with an easy question. "What do you do for fun?"

"Fun? I don't have time for fun. I hardly have time to sleep. I'm a grad student at Berkeley, and I teach two classes. I'm working on my dissertation, and I work fifty-plus hours a week at Black Rock."

I lean forward, resting my forearms on the table, my hands so close to hers, if I move just a fraction of an inch, we'd be touching. But I don't need to touch her to feel the heat rolling off her in waves. The same heat is rolling off me. "Can we go out? Dinner? Drinks? Whatever you want."

She looks down at the napkin in her lap. I see the crease between her brows. "I don't think that's a good idea."

That's not the answer I longed to hear, but it isn't a no. And it was more than I'd had yesterday. At least I know how to find her.

I can tell she wants to say more, so I wait. Finally, she admits, "I don't want you to not fund us because we're involved."

"That's smart, but that's not a good enough reason."

She closes her eyes and sighs. "Christopher, I can't. I've already told you how crazy busy I am right now, and your type is not good for me."

"What do you mean, 'my type'?"

"You're a player. You eat girls like me up."

"Oh, I'll eat you up, and you'll enjoy it. I can guarantee that."

She blushes, and I'm sure she's remembering how amazing I am at that. "You know what I mean."

"I don't know why you think I'm a player. I'm a good guy. I haven't had anyone serious in my life for a while. I'm not asking to marry you—yet—but I'd like to date you and see how it goes." It's embarrassing that I'm begging, but I don't care. I'm not going to let her studies—which I fully support—or our jobs be the reason we can't be together.

I need to remind her of what we have. I know I'm not the only one to feel this; she must feel it too. I lean over and tangle my hands in her hair as I pull her mouth toward me. Those tempting lips crash into mine. My tongue, rough and hot, dips into her mouth when she opens. She reaches for me and grasps my arms at the elbows. Dark flashes of arousal course through me, spreading through every limb and nerve ending, as my cock becomes rock-hard.

I let her go, and she sits back in her chair. "You don't take no for an answer, do you?"

"No. I won't put any more pressure on you than you already have." I throw cash on the table and reach for her hand. "But I will do whatever it takes to make it work."

"I need to get back to work. Dr. Johnson wasn't thrilled I was leaving so quickly after you."

"Do you think it's because I kicked him out of our meeting?"

"Yes. I have no doubt he sat in the next room and listened to every word. It's just the way he is—he wants to be in control. It's his name and reputation hanging out there."

We walk outside, and she pulls her phone out to schedule a ride. "I can drop you at the end of the block."

She looks conflicted but finally agrees.

When we arrive at the end of the block, I plead, "Can we please have dinner on Saturday night?"

She nods. "Text me."

chapter

ELEVEN

ISABELLA

When I return to the lab, it's quiet. "Where is everyone?" I ask Mindy.

"Dr. Johnson left right after you did, and a few people are at lunch or are in the lunch room."

I nod. "I'll be in my office if anyone needs me."

I sit in my chair and realize how shocked I am that I ran into Christopher. I thought about him almost every day since we were together. I can't believe our lives intersected. My grandmother would tell me that it is something worth checking out, but maybe I'm only trying to make it be something it isn't. I'll need to protect my heart.

Taking a deep breath, I look at the mounds of research to go through. I'm elbow deep into the numbers when my cell phone pings.

Christopher: Thanks for lunch today.

Christopher: I meant it when I said I was hoping to see you on Saturday night. Dinner at Farallon in Union Square?

I smile to myself. I can't help but flirt.

Me: Is there a reason you've picked the best raw oyster bar in the city?

Christopher: Is it working?

Me: It might. I can meet you there. Only dinner though. No dancing or anything else.

Christopher: Fine. I just want to spend time with you.

Me: I have to get back to work. I'm trying to develop a cure you know.

Christopher: 7, Saturday night at Farallon.

Me: I look forward to it.

And I am looking forward to seeing him again. Nothing can dash my mood, even now as I see Dr. Johnson heading my way.

"Ms. Vargas, where did you go after your meeting with Mr. Reinhardt?"

"I had lunch plans with a friend."

"You don't have time for lunch."

"It couldn't be avoided."

"I want a rundown on your progress today before you leave." He turns to leave and stops. "And you'd better put in a full day. As far as I can tell, you've done nothing today."

I look at his back as he strides out of my office. *Asshole.*

I throw myself into the data that the team has come up with so far, and I like what I'm seeing. Walking through each data point I'm given, I'm cautiously optimistic. It's after ten when I look up. I have a vague recollection of people telling me they were leaving for the night, but I didn't realize how long ago it was that they had left.

Printing the document, I send a copy to my cloud for use in my dissertation and put a copy on Dr. Johnson's desk. I'm teaching in the morning, but I'm excited to see his thoughts.

I call a rideshare home. This time of night, the homeless can overtake some of the buses, and normally, as long as I can keep my distance from the smell, I'm fine, but I'm more interested in getting home quickly tonight and without my senses being assaulted.

I lie in bed, willing the sandman to come and take me to dreamland, but my mind's too active. I think about running into Christopher. I'm excited about our flirtation over text. I can't help myself. It's after midnight, but I don't care.

Me: Good night, Christopher.

I watch the rotating dots telling me he's replying, and I'm anxious.

Christopher: Good night, Bella. Wish you were here.

Me: I look forward to Saturday night.

Christopher: Me too.

I don't respond, because I want to be more than just a booty call. At some point, I drift off, and my alarm is ringing. It's 5:00 a.m. *Why do I do this to myself?*

I slowly pull the covers off, and the cool air hits me. I'd rather crawl back under the covers and enjoy more of what my warm bed and the insides of my eyes have to offer, but I need to go for a run this morning before I get on the bus to make it for my nine o'clock class at Berkeley.

It's dark and cold outside. After pulling on a pair of sweatpants, a ratty old sweatshirt, and an orange safety vest, I'm ready to brave the morning drizzle. Popping my phone and a single house key in an armband, I head out. I used to listen to music as I ran, but after a mugging I read about in the paper, I don't want to be preoccupied and not pay attention to my surroundings. Plus it really gives me the chance to think without any distractions.

I run because it helps to center me. With everything I have going on, plus I'm adding Christopher to the mix, running helps me with my stress. Don't get me wrong, I hate every single minute of it, but it's how I find the way to get it all taken care of. I only run three miles, but I run up a forty-five-degree incline, and I'm convinced it's what helps me keep my big butt from getting bigger.

The streets begin to wake up at this time of the morning. The bakery on 18th Street is always so inviting. I can almost taste the sweet breads they're baking as the scent wafts through the air as I approach. It's quiet, except for the occasional car driving by or music playing in various apartments. Watching the lights in the apartments above the shops begin to light as I go reminds me of who might live in many of these homes. Professionals? Artists? Tech?

I grew up in this area, and what I love most about it is the abundance of color from the beautiful murals on the walls of the buildings on streets and alleys. My favorite is the MaestraPeace Mural, or Woman's Mural. It was painted on the Women's Building and honors women's contributions from around the world. It's an internationally recognized symbol of woman and all their beauty, power, and intellect. It's painted across two walls and covers the entire side of a building in bright, vivid colors. The mural is the result of a multicultural, multigenerational collaboration between seven women artists—one of which was my aunt. It makes me proud of my heritage and my neighborhood.

After a quick shower, I make the bus to Union Station on time and then the BART train over to Berkeley. It ends up taking about an hour and a half, but I use my time wisely and work through my notes to prepare for my lecture. Maybe having a car is overrated.

As I read about today's topic on cell regeneration, my mind slips to Christopher and what he looked like the morning I left him in bed. How delicious he looked with his curls framing his beautiful face, his chest bare and the sheets wrapped around his waist, hiding my new favorite toy.

My classes pass quickly, and I make it back to the lab just after noon, where I work until ten—which has become my daily routine—before heading home. Just as I'm settling in for bed, my phone pings.

Christopher: I hope you had a good day. Reservations are made for tomorrow night at 7. Good night, my angel.

Me: One more sleep. Good night.

I know I must fall asleep with a smile on my face. I must.

My cell phone pings again and a smile spreads across my face. I'm so lucky to have so many wonderful people in my life.

Ellie: Ferry Plaza farmers market this morning?

Me: If I can get coffee.

Ellie: Great. See you in an hour outside the coffee stand. Last one there buys.

Me: See you then.

I quickly put on yoga pants and a wool sweater and head out the door with my reusable bags and wallet. Ellie is always late. I'll have already bought the coffee for both of us by the time she gets there, but I don't care. She does so much for me.

Ellie arrives out of breath but looking perfectly coifed for something other than wandering the farmers market. I raise my eyebrow at her.

"What? You never know who you may meet." She shrugs and smiles broadly.

I roll my eyes.

"Any word on the meeting with the investor?" Ellie asks in an attempt to distract me.

"If you can believe it, the asshole met with him without telling me."

"Are you fucking joking? What are you going to do?"

"Believe it or not, the investor showed up on Wednesday to meet with me, and Dr. Johnson was none too happy. But—"

"I'll bet. That weasel! Bella, you need to watch that man like a hawk. There is something totally not right with him. This is your idea, and he's only secondary to the medication you're developing."

"I know that, but you'll never guess who the investor is."

"You know the investor?"

I nod. "It's Christopher from the night of your birthday party."

She stops and pulls my arm so we are facing one another. "You mean the god that took your chastity belt and threw it away?"

"Shh! Could you please try to be a bit discreet?" I beg as I see smirks from people walking by. "Yes, he's the one."

"I think that means that karma is telling you that you are not done with that boy yet."

I shrug. "We're going to dinner tonight."

She grabs me in a tight embrace. "That's awesome."

"Don't go planning any weddings. I'm nervous to get involved with him because I don't want that to be a reason he doesn't fund us."

"I get that. Just promise me you'll have fun."

"Promise. Now, I want to see what Jordana's Flowers has today. I'm in the mood for flowers in my apartment."

We pick a few items up as we walk and catch up. Jordana's is my favorite stall in the entire market. It's overflowing with flowers of every color and kind and smells divine.

I see plush clusters of white, pink, purple, and blue, and I bury my nose in the blooms, loving the heavenly scent.

Two women are standing and doing the same. One points and says, "Look, Emerson, white hydrangeas. They'd look perfect in the foyer at my mother's. What do you think?"

Her friend takes a big sniff. "I think she'd love them."

I've already picked up a stack of pink clusters and start collecting white forget-me-nots and some greens, putting my bouquet together.

The dark-haired woman turns to me and asks, "How did you do that?"

"Do what?" I'm perplexed by her question.

"How did you know that those little white flowers would go so well with the pink hydrangeas?"

I shrug. "I love the smell of the hydrangeas, and I love the look of the pink and the sprinkle of white."

"What would you put with the white flowers?"

Stepping back and surveying what Jordana has today, and I spot some small purple flowers. "What about these with these green leaves?"

"I love them."

Jordana comes over. "I see my favorite customers are finally meeting."

I smile and hand the woman the bouquet I just put together for her. "Hello, I'm Bella."

She takes the flowers. "Pleased to meet you. I'm Caroline."

It hits me who she is, and I feel beyond stupid. She's Caroline Arnault, a San Francisco celebrity. I feel an elbow in my side and quickly say, "Oh, and this is my best friend, Ellie."

Caroline motions to the woman beside her and says, "And this is my best friend, Emerson."

"You both have great eyes for flowers," Jordana chimes in.

"Well, given you have the most beautiful and unique selection each week, it's hard to not have a good eye," I tell her.

"Agreed." Turning to me, Caroline gushes, "I get so many compliments on her flowers each week. I love them. While you don't need her to put the bouquets together, she's also great at that too."

We chat a few moments longer before breaking away. "Did you recognize her?" Ellie asks once we're out of earshot.

"Of course I did. She's as close as you get to royalty here in the U.S."

"I read in a gossip website that she's dating the prince of Lichtenstein."

"She's beautiful and gracious. I'm sure she'd make a great queen one day."

"He's a playboy. His brother is the king. But she could be a princess," Ellie informs me.

Not one for gossip, I change the subject. "Oh, look at the size of that zucchini."

Ellie takes the hint, and we shop for another half hour before going our separate ways. I need to get some work done before I see Christopher tonight.

Several hours later, I'm buried in my data when my cell phone pings.

Christopher: Don't get so wrapped up in your work that you forget me tonight.

I laugh. How does he know me so well?

Me: Are you stalking me?

Christopher: No. I just understand how busy you are. I can pick you up, so you don't have to drive or pay for a ride tonight.

Me: I can meet you. It isn't a problem.

Christopher: I'll be there early in the bar. Let me know if you change your mind.

I look at the time and decide, since it's after five, I should begin to get ready. I race home and fill the bath with hot water and add jasmine and orange oils. I don't typically wear perfume, but these oils are my favorite.

I relax into the bath and fight off the stress. I'm becoming anxious about my date. I contemplate taking care of myself to help me relax, since I don't want to sleep with him tonight, but I decide against it. I shave my legs, pluck at my brows, moisturize my entire body, and play with my hair, making my unruly curls soft and cascading down.

I've been debating all week what I should wear. I decide to go with a lace dress that offers the illusion of skin-baring allure and ladylike and conservative refinement in a tea-length silhouette, pairing it with a cute strappy sandal.

For makeup, I go with a smoky eye and dark red lipstick. Carefully examining myself in the mirror, I decide I look as good as it's going to get—and I think I look pretty good.

When the rideshare drops me off in front of the restaurant at a quarter to seven, I stride into the crowded entry and enjoy the handblown glass sculptures on the ceiling, giving the illusion you are swimming beneath the jellyfish in the ocean. I spot him at the bar and walk over. He literally takes my breath away. Aesthetically, he is so damn perfect. His blond hair and striking hazel eyes, which seem to change from moment to moment, mesmerize me. His perfectly ripped body fills out the custom suit he is wearing beautifully. His broad shoulders and massive chest make me wish we were alone. I'm not sure I'll be able to control myself if he pushes too hard.

He opens his arms wide, and he embraces me. "You look stunning."

I blush from head to toe. "Thank you. Have you been waiting long?"

"No, I just got here and ordered our drinks."

"You did?"

"A white wine for you and scotch for me."

I must have a surprised look on my face, because he adds, "The first time we met, you were drinking white wine. If you don't want it, we can order you something else."

"No, that's exactly what I would have ordered. You're going to make this hard to separate business and pleasure, aren't you?"

He leans in, and his breath is warm on my ear. "Tonight is all about pleasure—not work."

My nipples pebble, and my core clenches. I'm a goner. Whatever he wants, I won't be able to resist. I've never felt this kind of pull with anyone before.

The bartender delivers our drinks, and after handing me mine, Christopher raises his glass. "To new adventures."

I smile and clink his glass. Taking a sip of wine, I'm stunned by the flavor. This is no ordinary two-buck chuck, which is what I usually drink. "This is an excellent wine."

"It's a Bellisima. One of the partners in my firm is married to a family member who runs the U.S. group of Bellisima wines. I've learned a lot from Andy about wine, so if I see it on a menu, I get it, and I'm never disappointed. It's really a fascinating story."

"Wow. Tell me about your company."

"We have all night to talk about them, and I hope to introduce you to them eventually."

"Okay then, what do you want to talk about?"

The hostess arrives with a tray in her hands to carry our drinks. "Mr. Reinhardt, your table is ready."

We hand over our drinks and follow her into a semiprivate room in the back.

"Are you celebrating anything special tonight?" she asks us as we follow her.

Christopher winks at me and smiles. "Yes. Our reunion."

"Very nice. Here's your table." As she places our drinks in front of us, she shares, "You will be served by Michael and Jean-Claude this evening. Can I offer you carbonated or still water for the table?"

Christopher looks at me and offers me the choice. "Carbonated please."

"I'll have the same."

We settle in, and I look across at him. He truly is handsome, but I don't know very much about him. "I guess we should back up and get to know one another a bit. Where are you from originally?"

"Minnesota. And you?"

"I grew up here in San Francisco, but I was born down in Los Angeles while my parents were in medical school."

"It's very rare to grow up here. What part of The City did you live?"

I chuckle. "The Mission. It's much more popular today with the hipsters, but it was the Hispanic neighborhood when I was growing up. It's my favorite." I take a sip of my water. "What about your family? Brothers? Sisters?"

"I have a brother and a sister. Both live within twenty minutes of my parents. What about you?"

"Just me. My mom was very focused on her career. My dad and I were close."

"He has Parkinson's?"

"Yes. He was my best friend growing up. I don't think what we are creating will help him, but it may help others."

When a tray of raw oysters arrives, I look at him in surprise.

"You did mention them in your text message. I know they are quite the aphrodisiac but no pressure. Honest."

"You're too much." When I reach for him, I feel the electricity between us. "Did you order anything else?"

"That's all I ordered. You can get the lobster if you'd like. Anything and everything on the menu."

I look the menu over carefully. "I think I'll go with the tuna. What looks good to you?"

"You mean other than you?"

I blush.

"Too much?" he asks, and I shake my head. "I'll probably go with the sea bass."

Jean-Claude arrives and asks us about the oysters.

While we eat, I ask, "Tell me about your company. Do you like the people you work with?"

"Very much. It was started by these three guys who had gone to undergrad together at Stanford. They each worked for various start-ups and made more money than they knew what to do with. This all started when they used their money to continue to invest in other start-ups, and they liked doing that rather than work for the companies they worked for, so they formed their own investment company."

"Sounds like they have the magic touch."

"Well, they've grown. They hired their lawyer, Sara, and Dillon heard Emerson speak at a conference, and bringing her and her company into SHN was a real game changer for them. What makes us different than any other VC company out there is that we tend to take over a lot of the operational side so that the company can focus on what they do right. And I'm one of three partners who go out and talk companies, like Black Rock, into allowing us to invest in them."

"I would think companies would line up around the block to allow you to invest in them."

"Many would, but not all companies want one large investor. That gives us a lot of say in how things are done. But in less than ten years, we've had over one hundred and fifty companies go public or were successfully sold, and our failure rate is under 10 percent."

"That must be why Dr. Johnson is so interested in you financing us."

"We have a lot of boxes to check before we go there."

I'm stunned by this comment. "Really? He seemed to think we'd have a check from you guys in a few weeks."

His eyes grow to saucers. "Um, no. If we move quickly, we might be there in six months."

"Wow. Why so long?"

"I still need to get more into your data, which I can't do until we sign a nondisclosure. If I believe it's a strong investment, I will pass it along to the technology team. Our technology team will work with someone to validate your conclusions. If it passes that hurdle, it goes to our finance team. They'll want to be sure we get a sound investment and determine our commitment. Once we can agree to that, it goes to our operations team. They will meet with you and Dr. Johnson and all your staff and do an evaluation. Sometimes we make suggestions of leadership changes."

The hair on the back of my neck stands on end. "Would you terminate partnership agreements?"

"Not necessarily. We've had founders that move to advisory roles. Much depends on their leadership styles." He reaches across the table and holds my hand while rubbing his thumb over my knuckles. "I'm only describing what we do in general. I can't say any of this will apply to Black Rock."

I nod, understanding what he's saying. "Are we allowed to talk to other venture capital firms? Could they come in and undercut you for money?"

"It's happened. But if you're doing it for timing, the standard due diligence for all venture capital firms is a minimum of six months out."

Our dinners arrive, and we talk about every topic I can think of, and it's a refreshing conversation. He appreciates my opinion, even when it's different, and he makes me laugh.

Clearing our plates, Jean-Claude asks, "Care for coffee or dessert tonight?"

"We'll take a look," I offer.

He leaves the dessert menus behind, and we look them over.

"Are you having fun tonight?" Christopher asks.

"I am. It's a welcome distraction from everything going on in my life."

"I'm not ready for tonight to end."

I sit back in my chair. If I'm honest with myself, neither am I. I wouldn't mind exploring things further, but I'm conflicted. "If we explore a personal relationship, will that preclude your company from investing in mine?"

"Honestly, I'm not sure. Our partnership agreements only define in-office relationships. But I'm incredibly interested in a personal relationship with you."

My heart beats faster, and in my mind, I'm doing a happy dance. "I'd be interested as well, but my company needs funding."

"I can tell you where I stand right now on funding Black Rock. I like what you're doing and think it would be a nice bonus to our portfolio. I plan on passing it along. I don't make the final decision to fund and, as I mentioned, you have several hurdles to pass. I think operationally is where you will struggle. Dr. Johnson may be a problem, but without him, you may struggle to get the name recognition needed to finance without your PhD."

I take in what he says. "Thank you for your honesty."

"Did I just ruin any chance of exploring a personal relationship?"

"I don't think so. I was thinking about dessert. What about you?"

"I thought I might have you for dessert."

The thought alone turns me on. I've very fond memories of the last time we were together. "Then maybe we should get the check and go somewhere more conducive to that." I'm shocked at how forward I'm being, but I can't help myself around him. I've had a great time, and I want more.

• • •

He pays the check, and as we wait for a rideshare, he lowers his mouth to mine. He kisses me softly, and I open my mouth with a low moan, wanting more of Christopher—all of Christopher.

"We can go to your place or mine, but the rule is we are having breakfast tomorrow morning."

"I will have to do some work tomorrow."

"Do you want to pick up whatever you need from your place and stay at mine?"

I like the sound of that, so we swing by my apartment and pick up an overnight bag, my work, and study things for tomorrow.

We make out in the car like teenagers, getting my motor running. When we arrive at Christopher's place, he carries my things inside and drops them by the door before pushing me up against the wall. His hands explore me. I want this so bad.

He removes my dress, letting it pool at our feet. "You're so beautiful," he murmurs. His mouth covers mine as he continues his exploration.

I pull his tie and begin to unbutton his shirt, trying hard not to break our kiss. I slide his heavily starched shirt over his shoulders and drop it on top of my dress.

He traces the outline of the lace of my bra and runs his fingers over my nipples as they harden and ache for more attention. "I love how receptive your body is to my touch." He bends down and bites at my nipples through the thin satin.

His belt is my next goal. "I get my dessert too, don't I?"

"You can have as many servings of dessert tonight as you want," he growls.

I unbuckle his pants, and they fall to the floor. His cock escapes his boxers as I slink my hand around his hardness. I moan at the sight of it, the feel of it, the same way I did the last time we were together. "You make me so hot," I say as his hand slides into my panties, his fingers finding my opening. When I massage his balls, he moans in my mouth. He grabs me by the hand and leads me into his living room. .The floor-to-ceiling windows overlooking the bay are majestic, but more exciting to me is what is hidden inside his boxer briefs, so I slide them off his hips. He's beautiful.

"You're first. I've been craving this pussy ever since you left me—which you will be punished for this evening." I sit down on the black couch, the coolness of the leather juxtaposed to how hot I'm feeling. He opens my legs wide, exposing me completely, and his other hand begins to softly finger my folds. I'm already dripping. He leans down and takes a long and luscious lick which lights me on fire.

He's so hard it makes me want to fuck him until I can't see straight.

His hands explore as he kisses down my taut stomach. When he reaches the top of my pussy, I grab the sides of his face and try to stop him. I want to pleasure him, but he has other ideas. Laying back, I relax and take in his ministrations.

Taking a deep sniff of my scent, he dips his face down between my legs and licks me from one end of my slit to the other, from bottom to top. His tongue drags across my hard clit, which is so swollen it almost feels like it'll burst. He does it a few times before finally taking it between his lips and sucking it into his mouth. He runs his tongue back and forth across it quickly, and I wrap my fingers in his hair, pressing his face into me so hard it's a miracle he can breathe.

My breathing becomes labored, my hips moving involuntarily, and I fist the accent pillows around me. "I'm going to come!"

He inserts his fingers into my tight canal and thrusts them in and out while his tongue strums my clit. I moan my satisfaction, and even if only for a moment, he looks content.

He wipes his chin of my juices as his other hand reaches across to his wallet on the side table, retrieving a condom package. I watch as he rips it open with his teeth and rolls it on.

"Are you ready?" he asks.

I nod, not sure of what to expect. Christopher's much bigger, and I was pretty sore for a few days after last time. It was a good kind of sore.

He teases me, rubbing his hard cock over my throbbing clit before entering, moving slowly for a few seconds, giving me time to adjust to his size. Once I'm stretched comfortably around him, he begins to move faster, plunging in and out of me. The look of ecstasy on his face is almost as sexy as the feeling of him inside me.

Each stroke pulls out another level of pleasure until I'm sure I'm going to pass out. He's moaning and panting as he picks up his pace, and I claw at his back, sure to be leaving scratch marks in my wake. I wrap my legs around his body, his hands everywhere as he slams into me repeatedly. He closes his eyes and lifts his chin as he locks in place above me, crying out loudly. I take control of our sex and work him as best I can from beneath him, needing to watch him come undone. He cries out again, and I come from the intense pressure mixed with the deliciously hot sounds of him taking what he needs from me.

Limp with exhaustion, we lie here for a few minutes with Christoper resting against me. I run my fingers through his sweat-slicked hair and over his back. I can't help but kiss the side of his face over and over again. Our limbs are intertwined, our bodies as close as they can be, reassuring ourselves and each other as we attempt to catch our breath.

We're both sweaty and raw, and just so well-fucked. He falls beside me on the couch, takes my hand, kisses it, and holds on tight. I turn my face to his, our foreheads touching, our hearts beating in unison. "Don't let me go."

"Never," Christopher says. And I believe him.

chapter

TWELEVE

CHRISTOPHER

My cell phone rings, and I see it's my buddy, Dave. "Hello?"

"Dude, you up for a game of basketball this evening and hitting Scotty's Bar afterward? Say around six thirty?"

"As long as Greg isn't playing tonight. I'm still nursing a bruise on my hip that he gave me. It's putting a crimp in my style with Bella."

"I heard you met some girl," he teases.

"I did, and she could be the one." I say that with so much confidence that I realize I'm speaking the truth.

"Mr. Right Now is thinking he may have found Miss Right?"

"It's still early, but she hits everything on my list."

"You can tell us all about her during our game."

"Are you kidding? You might try to snake her out from under me. No way. I'm telling you, so you don't try to get me to go home with some warm body tonight at Scotty's."

"Fine. I was raised to share. You can be that way. See you at the Y."

I do not share. Absolutely not. No way. I know he's teasing me, so I let it go. "Ciao."

I hang up to go back to studying and preparing my presentation on Black Rock for Sunday night at our meeting. I like the data and their goals and think they would be great for two big pharmas I've sold to in the past. At some point, I'm going to have to come clean about my relationship with Bella. I don't want it to affect anything, and I want to keep this on the up and up.

I pull out my partnership agreement and read the clause about personal relationships. It says I need to inform the managing partner if I have a personal relationship with an SHN employee, a client, or a prospective client. *Fuck.*

I instant message Mason from our intranet.

Me: Hey, you got a second?

Mason: Sure, come on in.

I wander to his office and sit across from him. "I'm preparing my presentation for Sunday night on Black Rock Therapeutics."

"How are they looking?"

"I'd say pretty decent. I'm going to refer them on. I should tell you, I met a girl a few weeks ago, and we started dating."

He looks at me and a crinkle forms between his eyes, signaling he's puzzled by the sharing of my personal life. "She works for Black Rock and is the person behind the idea. Up until recently, I had always talked to Dr. Vance Johnson, and he never introduced us or even spoke about her. Bella and I randomly met at a club, and I approached her when some guy was too friendly and wouldn't take a hint. It's truly a coincidence. My partnership agreement tells me I'm to notify you of the relationship."

The crinkle goes away. "Okay. Who is she in relation to the organization?"

"Dr. Johnson refers to her as his research assistant, but she's the co-founder and is a PhD candidate at Berkeley. This idea came from her dissertation."

"But Dr. Vance Johnson is leading this?"

"Yes."

"How do you feel about the investment?"

"Well, I don't want to shade anyone's opinion, but I think Dr. Johnson is a weasel. I like her, and honestly, I'm not going to try to influence this, but she's the brains behind this. He couldn't explain her data or where they were in vetting their process. He worked hard to keep us separate, but I showed up, expecting to meet a man and it was her. The idea is solid, and the research seems legit. I will let Emerson make any personnel decisions."

"This is the woman you mentioned at dinner—you met her and didn't get her information."

"That's her. I was shocked when I found her at Black Rock."

Mason looks at his hands, which are crossed in front of him, and is silent a few moments. Then he shrugs. "Okay, consider me informed. You don't have to share that fact on Sunday night and hopefully one of these Sundays you can bring her to dinner at the Arnaults'. Annabelle would love to have someone else to hang out with."

I'm not sure I want Annabelle anywhere near Bella; she might turn her into a stuck-up bitch.

"I hear ya. All right then, I'll get back to it." I return to my office and feel good that I'm not doing anything underhanded or tricky.

When six o'clock rolls around, I pack up and head to the Y. It's the best basketball court in the city, and over time I've met a bunch of guys who are similar in skill level, and we will play against one another for a workout a few nights a week.

I see my buddy Dave. "Hey. You ready to get your ass kicked?"

"Dream on, dude. You're going down," he teases.

I love that we can joke about basketball. We're both huge college hoops fans, but I tend to be a Carolina fan while he pretends to be a Michigan fan—a far lesser college basketball team.

While we dress, we talk a little bit about college basketball and where the NCAA's will be this year and who might be going pro.

We walk into the courts and are told which team we are on, and we play hard for over an hour and a half—no talking about Bella, our jobs, or college teams. It's a great workout, and after we're done, we hit the showers. I think about Bella and wouldn't mind trying to catch up with her tonight. I don't want to push her. I know she has a lot on her plate, and I don't want to be another hassle for her.

Scotty's Bar isn't far from the Y. It's crowded with the downtown hipsters, but we score a table in a good spot. "What'll you have?"

Dave looks at me and considers his options. "I was thinking the microbrew they have on tap."

"I've got the first round." After placing my order, I check out the bar. There are some cute girls, but I'm not really interested in any of them. At the table next to Dave, I see a woman who looks familiar. I can't quite figure out what it is about her. She has dark hair, huge dark brown eyes, and a cute figure. She's not as beautiful as Bella, but she's definitely beautiful. It hits me like a thunderbolt. I think she's the birthday girl from the night I met Bella.

I pay for our beers and take them to my table. I can't help myself. I stop at her table. "Hi, I'm Christopher Reinhardt. Aren't you friends with Isabella Vargas?"

She looks me over carefully. "Yes, have we met?"

"I think we met at The Church for your birthday party? I became friends with Bella that night."

"Oh, you're *that* Christopher?"

I'm not sure what Bella has said to her friend. "I guess I would be *that* Christopher. What's your name?"

"Elinor Richardson, but you can call me Ellie."

"Great to officially meet you."

I see Dave checking Ellie out, but he sits and just watches.

"You know, you really knocked her off her feet," she informs me. "I'm really grateful to you for making her have a personal life."

"Well, I think I should be thanking you for having a birthday party and getting her out."

"I like the way you think, Christopher." She looks over at Dave and smiles.

"Here, let me introduce you to my friend. This is Dave Marshall. He and I went to school together, but I should warn you, he's a Michigan basketball fan."

"Hi, nice to meet you. Call me Ellie, and I'm a Duke fan." I groan internally, knowing she's going to hate me in a few seconds.

"Ellie, I love you already. Christopher went to medical school at Carolina," Dave gushes.

She groans. "That's disappointing. He'll have to break up with Bella then."

While they're giving me a hard time, I look up, and who do I see? Annabelle and some woman. I don't know what's worse, hearing how great Duke and Michigan are or talking to Annabelle and her friend. I guess I don't have a choice when they march up to our table.

"Christopher!" She gives me a hug that lasts a few seconds too long and kisses me on each cheek. From the corner of my eye, I see Ellie stand back and watch me carefully.

"Annabelle, so good to see you. Let me introduce you to my friends. This is Ellie and Dave. Ellie is my girlfriend's best friend." I see Ellie visibly relax. "And Dave and I went to the University of Minnesota together." Turning to Ellie and Dave, I explain, "Annabelle is the girlfriend to the managing partner at my firm, Mason Sullivan."

She preens like a peacock. "And this is my friend Amanda. It's so wonderful to see you someplace other than that boring dinner on Sunday nights. I've wanted to introduce the two of you."

"Nice to meet you, Amanda." Turning to Annabelle, I say, "You know, if you don't like Sunday night dinners, it isn't mandatory for you. You don't have to come. I'm not sure I'd enjoy them if I didn't work for SHN."

"Mason requires it, so I go and pretend to have a good time. They're just dreadful."

She's not a very good actress. Everyone knows she doesn't enjoy these dinners.

I smile and nod. I don't know what to say to her.

"How serious is it with your girlfriend?" Annabelle asks. Ellie is still watching me and waiting to hear my answer. It's definitely piqued her curiosity.

"It is serious. I'm quite smitten."

"Oh, that's too bad. I think you're really missing out with Amanda," she singsongs to tempt me. It doesn't work.

"What brings you here to Scotty's Bar? You don't seem the type to slum it."

She doesn't get my dig. "We're meeting a couple of friends for drinks. Do you come here often?"

"Sometimes after we play basketball at the Y."

"That's nice." She points to a tall blond man who's just walked in. "There they are."

She waves, and he walks over. "This is Christopher. He works with Mason."

I extend my hand. "Nice to meet you." He doesn't share his name, and I find it a little odd. "My friends are over there." He points to a group of less-than-savory-looking characters and wanders off. Apparently, he has no manners.

I'm ready to ask his name when Annabelle says, "Well, I'll see you on Sunday night."

"See you then."

I turn back to Dave and Ellie, finding them deep in conversation about college basketball. Dave's a goner. They are hitting it off, and I'm kind of starting to feel like a third wheel.

I text Bella.

Me: You'll never guess who I ran into?

Bella: Who?

Me: Ellie. We're here at Scotty's Bar downtown.

Bella: Don't let her tell any stories about me. All she tells are lies. :)

I look up at Ellie. "I just told Bella that I ran into you, and she says you're not allowed to tell me any stories. Apparently, 'all you tell are lies.'"

Ellie laughs and says, "You tell her I'm telling the story about what happened to us in 10th grade."

I typed out Ellie's threat.

Bella: If she even thinks about telling you that story, tell her she will be dead to me and I mean it. Dead.

I read the text out loud to Ellie, and she laughs. "It's really not that entertaining of a story. It's just really funny at her expense."

Me: She's going to tell me the story. Better be ready. I'm going to lord it over you for the rest of our lives.

Bella: I swear to God, I'm going to kill her.

Me: It's all lies anyway. Why would I believe her over you to start with?

Bella: I knew there was a reason to like you.

Me: That's the only reason?

Bella: I can think of a few more.

Me: Well, I can think of a lot of other reasons. I'll be happy to show you. What are you doing tonight?"

Bella: Working. What else is new?

Me: I just played basketball with my buddy Dave from undergrad, and I'd love to see you tonight if you want to get together???

Bella: To have sex?

Me: Well, that'd be a bonus, but I'm happy to watch a movie, go to dinner, paint your toenails... whatever it takes just to spend time with you.

Bella: Paint my toenails?

Me: Whatever it takes.

Bella: I'll see what I can do.

Me: Let me know what you decide. I'm going to hang out here for a little bit with Ellie and Dave before I head home. You're welcome to meet me here, my place, or of course I can pick you up in Berkeley or wherever you're at. I'd just love to see you.

Dave and Ellie seem to be getting along really well, so after another drink, I decide to head home. I say my goodbyes and wave across the bar to Annabelle.

As I ride home in a rideshare, I text Bella to tell her I'm headed home, but I can meet her wherever. I sound desperate, and maybe I am. It's been two days since I've seen her, and I want to look into her big, dark brown eyes.

Bella: Give me 20 minutes, and I'll meet you at your place. Are you up for dinner?

Me: Dinner would be great. Order in or go out?

Bella: Order in something simple. Pizza or something. Whatever you want.

Me: Other than you for dinner, I'll take any scraps I can get.

Bella: 20 minutes.

There's a really good pizza place not too far from where I live, and I order up a pizza with everything on it with a nice thick crust. I open a beer and try not to get too anxious. When my doorbell rings, I'm excited but also calm knowing she's arrived. Opening the door, I see her standing there in a pair of jeans and a blue sweater that hugs all the right places. She takes my breath away. "You made it."

She leans in, her soft lips touching mine, and I swear my cock is hard already.

"I brought my overnight bag. I hope that's okay."

"Of course it is. I'll take whatever time I can get from you—even if its sleeping next to you. Pizza will be here in about ten minutes."

"Is it okay to tell you I'm exhausted?"

I'm not sure if she's testing me, but I don't care. "We don't even have to have sex tonight. I'd love to hold you and spend the evening with you and just be together."

"Everything is overwhelming right now, but I'm glad to have you to spend time with."

chapter THIRTEEN

ISABELLA

"You do realize that you're late again today," Dr. Johnson bellows when I arrive.

"Dr. Johnson, as a reminder, this semester I teach class on Mondays, Wednesdays, and Fridays in Berkeley at nine and ten. I come in after I'm done with my class schedule."

"Ms. Vargas, that isn't what was discussed. You need to be better at setting an example for your staff. Where are you with analyzing the data? We need to be able to move on to the next phase of our study."

"I agree. I'll check in with Jim." I stop and say in a low voice, "Dr. Johnson, this is all set up in your contract with me. As a reminder, you're a 49 percent owner of this company. I own the majority share, and you work for me. I won't tolerate your insubordination."

He steps back, not liking to be reminded of who the boss around here ultimately is. "We need to have a discussion about the contracts, but I don't have time for that now. I need to know where you are with the data. Everyone is waiting for you. This is completely unacceptable behavior."

That man is going to drive me absolutely apeshit. I'm spread too thin, and I have too many things going on. Black Rock is doing great, and we're ahead of schedule. We've got SHN looking at us and seeming pleased with what we're doing. It looks like they're going to give us the money and will help set up for what I hope is an advancement in the treatment of Parkinson's. Today it takes over 2.5 million dollars to get a new drug developed, tested, and to market. We need SHN to get us there. Plus, I like that the SHN operations team might be able to control Dr. Johnson much better than I seem to be able to. What is his deal anyway?

I put my bag down inside my office and look around the lab. It's a ghost town. Where is everyone? Walking back to reception, I see Dr. Johnson is still there. "Where is everybody?"

"I don't know, and I don't care," he grumbles, obviously still smarting over my reprimand. Whatever. Act like you're seven. *You don't care about them, but you care about me? What the hell?*

"Okay, thanks." It isn't worth the fight. He runs the day-to-day operations, and I need him here. I head back to my office and open the file on the cloud drive. I notice that half the experiments that were supposed to be completed by today are incomplete. I wander over to my lab manager's office, finding it dark, but run into one of the lab techs in the hall. "Gayle, do you know where Jim is?"

She doesn't look at me or make any eye contact. "No, he quit."

"Quit? When did he quit?" I'm stunned. Why didn't he call me and tell me he was quitting, or why didn't Dr. Johnson tell me knowing full well that Jim is an integral part of our research.

"I don't know. He told Dr. Johnson, and he walked him out the door immediately."

"Why isn't anybody telling me these things?" I muse aloud.

She looks at me with a bored look. "I have no idea." She turns away and goes back to whatever she's doing. I'm not completely clear what her job is here, but I don't have the time to figure it out right now.

Rolling up my sleeves, I look around the lab and determined there are a few things that I can do to keep things going. I've worked in labs for almost five years. Doing research requires you to document the hell out of everything. It takes me a little over an hour to figure out where Jim was with the experiments and our initial trials. Now I know what needs to be done next.

By the time I'm finally getting the data, I look at my watch. It's been four hours and my stomach growls. I have a fleeting thought of having dinner with Christopher, but then Dr. Johnson comes into the lab. "What are you doing in here? Why aren't you going through the data?"

I look at him and wonder how he thinks data is acquired. "When you chose to walk Jim out after he quit, he didn't finish what he was doing. There was no data for me to analyze, so I have to pick up his job until we replace him. Why did Jim quit anyway?"

"Who knows, who cares? And we can't afford to replace him anytime soon."

"I care, and I'm curious why you decided to walk him out as soon as he resigned instead of trying to figure out if there was something we could do to keep him. He's vital to this project. He's been with me since the beginning."

"It doesn't matter. Get it done. We need to be ready to show our results during a meeting with the investors."

"I thought SHN was already up to speed?"

"We're probably not going to go with them. They're going to want to be too involved in our business, and they don't understand biotech. We'll never be successful under them."

"Deciding how much equity to take on is a joint decision that you and I will make. I'm not sure that they're out of play. I'm interested in how they run things over there."

"How do you know?"

"Because I did some research, and the success rate of their investments either being sold or purchased is well over 90 percent, which is 20 percent higher than any of their competitors."

"I think we'll do some angel funding that I'm looking at. We'll see what happens. I'm not committing to anybody. I have a good idea here, and everybody's going to beg us for this information to be part of this amazing cure for Parkinson's."

What did he just say? "*You* have a good idea?"

"Yes. You'd be playing in your lab across the bay if it wasn't for me."

I nod while I consider how I'm going to respond in such a way that I don't end up pummeling him to the ground. "I'd think twice about how you speak to me and how you treat our team." *Just because you won the Lasker Award, and all of those that have won the Lasker before are shoo-ins for a Nobel prize doesn't mean anything. You're such a fucking ass.*

My cell phone pings soon after six.

Christopher: Hey, you want to get together tonight?

Me: Can't. Overwhelmed, and I got in late for work since today is a teaching morning. Somebody quit in the office. And I have to be ready to do my own work tomorrow, as well as try to get caught up here at Black Rock.

Christopher: No pressure from me. If you change your mind, even if you just want to come and cuddle, I'm good with that. No sex required.

Bella: Thanks, I'll keep you posted.

I just don't have time for a relationship. I don't know what's going to happen. I run my hands through my hair, and there are more strands than normal laced in my fingers. Now I can worry about becoming bald. The stress is incredibly high, and I don't know how to minimize it except to just take it one thing at a time.

It's after nine, and I walk to our kitchen to stretch my legs and take a break. I need some caffeine. The office is deserted. Looking around, I notice coffee in the pot. It's cold, and I'd bet it was probably made this morning and is tar at this point, but maybe it's enough to keep me going. I pour it into a mug and put it in the microwave to heat. Not my first choice, but it will check all the boxes—hot and caffeine.

I hear my phone ringing in my office, so I return to answer it. "Hello?"

"Sweetheart, it's your mom." I roll my eyes like I'm fifteen again. Of course, I recognize her voice. "Where are you?"

"I'm at the lab trying to get through some things before I can head home. My lab manager quit."

"Why did he quit? Is your team having to keep these crazy hours you're keeping?"

"No, Mom. I don't know why he quit. I wasn't here when he gave his resignation. He just walked out the door and kind of left us holding in the bag."

"I'm sorry. That's never good. I just wanted to remind you that we have your cousin's birthday party coming up. Maria hasn't received your RSVP, and I wanted to make sure you were going to be there. Alejandra's really counting on you."

"I haven't RSVP'd, but I plan on being there. What's really going on? I always do my best to be at family events. What's everybody worried about?"

"You know it's a chance for us to bring the whole family together. Your grandmother is getting old, and we want everyone there for Alejandra and her."

"I promise, Mom, I'll be there. But you do know that the only thing Alejandra and I have in common right now is that we are cousins. She's sixteen, and I'm twenty-five. She couldn't care less about me being there—you do know that, right?"

"Yes, sweetheart, she probably doesn't care about you being at her party, but your aunt and I care about you. We're worried that you're just spending all of your time working and not out there dating or having fun."

"Actually, I've started seeing somebody. His name is Christopher. He went to medical school and works for a venture capital fund."

"How is his Spanish?"

"I haven't asked. We speak only English to one another." Trying to put my annoyance in check, I add, "And I find it funny that you are worried about my work ethic when I inherited my drive to work hard from you."

"Yes, and I look at what it has done for me. I thought I'd have plenty of years later with your father, and now he's sick and I'm all by myself."

"You're not by yourself. You have your sister and me. And you can rest assured that I'm dating Christopher. It's early but a nice relationship. We're taking it slow."

"Good," she says with conviction. "I'll look forward to meeting him at Alejandra's party."

I roll my eyes. I know that this is a losing battle to argue with her. "I'll ask him, but he may think it's a little early in our relationship to be meeting fifty family members."

"If he wants a future with you, he'll want to meet the family."

"I'll ask him. I'd better go if I want to get out of here before two." I'll broach the subject with Christopher. What a way to make him run away from me. He may not want to be overwhelmed by all of my crazy family.

I finally get the cup of coffee from the microwave. It's hot and strong and gives me enough energy to make it for a few more hours before I head home. When my day is done, and only toothpicks will keep my eyes open, I take a rideshare home. On the way, I see the late-night crowd enjoying the dance clubs and bars. I also see some of the locals keeping tabs on their blocks. Not long ago, this neighborhood was filled with gangs, and today I see the quiet of a sleeping family neighborhood. I grew up here. This is the heart of the Hispanic community, and there's so much activity going on in the bright and vivid colors. I love it all.

I wonder if this is something that Christopher would enjoy. It's too early to tell if he even wants to stay in San Francisco or move to his home in Minnesota. I barely even know him, and I'm not sure whether or not he'd be interested in anything long term, but it's worth trying to find out.

Just the thought of him gets my panties wet. My finger hovers over my phone, debating on whether or not I should text him. Its almost midnight. It's awfully late, and it would probably seem like a bootie call. And I know if I go over and spend the night with him, I won't make it tomorrow to my workout. That's always the first thing I drop, and it's the one thing that helps me with my stress.

It's such a tough decision, but then I think of his cute dimples, and I can't resist.

Me: Just leaving the lab. Sleep well.

Christopher: I've missed you tonight.

Me: I miss you too. Crazy day.

I take a big breath, deciding I'd rather ask over text than in person so he can easily turn it down without me having to see the conflict on his face.

Me: My cousin is turning sixteen. My family is planning a party on Saturday night. Let me know if you'd be interested in coming. No pressure—I promise. It's a lot of family, so I totally get it if you don't want to go.

I watch the dots rotate, and I'm surprised at his quick response.

Christopher: You know I'll go wherever you need or want me to go as long as I'm with you.

My heart beats triple time, and I have a smile on my face that nothing could wipe off.

Me: I guess if you wanted to come over to my place for a change, you're welcome to tonight.

Christopher: I'm on my way.

chapter

FOURTEEN

CHRISTOPHER

I'm not at all surprised that Bella lives in the Mission District. It's a great Latino district that is well-known and influential for its restaurants. There are dozens of great taquerias located throughout the neighborhood that showcase Mexican food, but there's also Salvadoran, Guatemalan, and Nicaraguan restaurants, and it's just a fun place to be, with bright murals and an eclectic and diverse community—everything from the tech people to long-term Latino residents. It has gentrified, but it still has some sketchy areas.

When the rideshare pulls up to her place, I see it's your typical San Francisco neighborhood house. It's a building that has been converted from a large house into three apartments. There is a garage out front that sits right up against a sidewalk that borders the street. Each house fills the property line to the edge so that the block looks like one long group of townhomes. No grass is visible from the front. Each of the units is on their own floor of the building—one behind the garage and one each on the second and the third floors.

Bella's home is the middle apartment. I ring the bell, and she buzzes me in. I can't help but feel butterflies in my stomach. I'm so excited to see her as I climb the stairs. I hear her open the door, and she's standing there in a pair of sleep shorts and a camisole. She looks beautiful, and her face lights up when she sees me, making me feel invincible.

"Welcome to the Mission. How do you like slumming?"

"Slumming? This place is great. I love it over here. There's so much diversity, and some of my favorite restaurants are here—the La Palma Mexicatessen, La Taqueria, and there's Foreign Cinema down the street."

"I grew up at La Palma. Anna and I went to school together. It was her parents' place, and she owns it now. It's a favorite of mine. I've been going there since I was a little girl."

"Is this the apartment you lived in when you were growing up?" I take in her studio apartment and hope that she grew up in a bigger place than this small apartment. But the apartment is quintessentially her. It has a bed with bright colors, a table covered in books and papers, a television on the wall, and small kitchen.

"No, I grew up a few blocks away above Delores Park. My mom sold it a few years ago to move closer to her job, my dad, and her sister down in San Jose. I can't imagine living in any other part of the City, or the Bay Area for that matter."

She lights up as she talks about her neighborhood, but I can see the circles under her eyes, and I realize she's struggling to stay awake. I reach for her and bring her in for a tight hug and a deep kiss. It's slow and passionate. "It's late. How about we get you in bed? You look exhausted, and I imagine you have an early morning."

"I might be insulted if you weren't telling me the truth." She reaches for my hand and leads me around her apartment while she turns lights off and gives me the tour. "Here is the bathroom in case you need that later. If I snore too loud, you can sleep on the couch."

"You don't snore."

"According to Ellie, I do."

"You purr in your sleep. I'll be fine."

"I was planning on getting up and going for a run in the morning. My stress levels are really high right now and starting my day off running seems to help."

"Can I join you?" She's talked about running in the mornings before, so I packed running shoes and workout gear in my overnight.

"Do you run?"

"I've been known to do some running. I tend to play basketball pick-up games these days for my workouts, but I was on the cross-country team in high school. There's a good chance you will lap me or just leave me in your dust if you're a sprinter, but I might be able to keep up with you."

"I'll set the alarm. I'm not a three-minute miler. I just need to get out and pound the pavement a little bit to just work through the stress."

"I get it. What time do you want to get up?"

"How about five thirty?"

I groan internally, knowing that time is quickly approaching. "That works." We move into her bed.

I strip down to my boxer shorts and crawl in between the sheets, and she cuddles right in with me. It just feels so right. She fits perfectly spooned in close to me. Almost immediately, her breathing becomes rhythmic, and I drift off quickly myself.

When the alarm goes off, I'm disoriented, and it takes me a minute to realize where I am. I was in such a deep sleep. I think we touched all night long. I'm not usually a cuddler. This woman is upending everything.

I hold her tight, not wanting to get right out of bed.

"If I question it, or if I go back to sleep, I may never get up. I need to get going. You don't have to come with me," she says sleepily.

I shake the cobwebs from my brain. "No, I need to do this."

We both quickly dress, and we're out the door. As we stretch a little bit on the sidewalk out front, she explains her running route.

I nod, and we start heading south on Mission Street. The traffic is light, and with the exception of a few breakfast spots and bakeries, the street is quiet. We run about eight blocks, and just as the neighborhood starts to get a little dicey, she turns right and runs uphill to the top of Dolores Park. My lungs are burning, and the only thing that keeps me going is hearing her breathing just as hard as I am.

Dolores Park is popular for a lot of reasons, but often when there is a park scene or picture where they want the San Francisco skyline in the background, this is where it's taken. This morning it is more beautiful than most because the sun is rising, and behind downtown and the sky is a contrast between the black night sky and the orange sun pushing her way into the darkness.

After twenty minutes of running, we arrive back at her place, and as we're cooling down, I notice I'm definitely breathing much harder than she is. She turns to me and says, "I'm impressed. You did pretty well for not running recently."

"Thanks. If I told you the truth that I hadn't been running in almost five years, would you believe me?"

She grins widely at me. "Not at all."

"Well good, because it's true; I haven't been running in almost five years, so I'm thankful to you for going probably a little slower than usual to let me stay with you."

"I'm grateful to have you join me for my run. I won't deny that there are some less-than-desirable locations in the Mission, but we turned before it gets too crazy, with the homeless and a methadone clinic. It makes me feel safer having you with me. Plus, I like the company, even if we didn't talk."

Once we enter the apartment, she offers, "Why don't you get in the shower first, and I'll get the coffee ready and check my emails so we can get out of here. I've got to get over to Union Station and on the BART for a nine o'clock class in Berkeley."

"No problem. I'll be quick." I jump in the shower, and it smells like her. I like her floral-smelling shampoo and her basic Ivory soap. I quickly realize I actually feel really great having just run. I have a ton of energy, and it's so early I can get several things on my to-do list crossed off.

Drying myself off, I alert her, "The shower's all yours."

I rub my hair with a towel and look up just in time to see the flash of her nakedness, and it takes all of my willpower to not act upon it and join her in the shower.

We are like a well-oiled machine and seem to alternate well in her small bathroom. When we are finally ready to catch our ride, we head downstairs. I look at her, and my heart almost stops. She's hardly wearing any makeup. Her hair is damp, and she's already distracted by her day. Our ride drops her at Union Station and then drops me at my office.

I arrive early, which is kind of nice. I'm not the first to arrive, and I noticed that Mason is here but behind closed doors. I don't want to interrupt anything, so I go in search of a cup of coffee and work my way through the *SVBJ*. Each morning I look to see what is going on with my clients and some prospects, and I know a few articles will be written about some emerging pharmaceutical companies, which tend to be my sweet spot.

The noise of the office slowly increases as more people arrive. I'm working through my presentation on Black Rock when my internal office instant message pings.

Mason: Can you come in here, please?

Me: I'll be right there.

Picking up my Moleskine notebook and pen, I walk to his office. Sitting with Mason is Sara, Cameron, Dillon, and Jim, our security guy. *This can't be good.*

"Hey, what's going on?"

"Well, apparently Evernote was hit by our hackers last night," Mason informs me.

I sit back hard in my chair and let out a big sigh of air. *Oh fuck.*

"So, what does that mean?" I ask. Evernote came to SHN because of a relationship with Dillon, and they were incredibly generous to assign them to me.

"It looks like they got into their human resources system and hijacked all their employee names, addresses, socials, and all their personal information, along with the credit card information from all their clients," Mason shares.

"My team has already gone onto the dark web, and we see the information up for sale," Jim adds.

"Oh crap. Does Evernote have to report this to someone?" I ask.

"It's the smart thing to do, but there's a lot of gray area in reporting requirements. Sara, you would know this better than I do—what do you think?" Mason asks.

"I'll have to look that up. I'm not sure really," Sara replies. "We'll do some research. There's the possibility that they may not have to report it."

"Jesus Christ. When is this going to end?" Dillon pleads to the ceiling.

I agree, this is just too much. "Who should I get in touch with at Evernote?"

Mason says, "Right now, Emerson is already on her way there to sit with her team member who works on-site. Because of it being the HR portal, Jim has her doing some covert research."

"Okay, what can I do to help? What do you need from me?"

Mason lets out a long breath. "You know, I don't know that there's anything we can do right now. They're your client, and we wanted you to know, but I think it's mostly up to Cameron and his team and Jim."

Cameron has been quietly listening to us. "I don't know if I'll put Parker on it again. He was pretty busy with Pineapple Technologies, and that's just wrapping up. I'll see where he's at and if he's open to working on Evernote." He looks at Jim. "Should I reach back out to Cora Perry at the FBI and see what her thoughts are and how she would like us to move forward?"

The room collectively seems to agree with Cameron's idea.

"Jim, do you have any different thoughts on what I can do?" Cameron asks.

Jim shrugs. "I think you're doing what's correct. You can check with Cora and see if she thinks we should pull Assistant US Attorney Walker Clifton in on this since we do know that it's our Adam and Eve."

Adam and Eve are two hackers who have been targeting us and our investments along with some of the other venture capital funds throughout the Bay Area. We recently discovered their names in a major breach of a different client, and the US attorney's office was able to secure multiple indictments against them.

The meeting begins to break up. I feel helpless. I don't have anything to do other than sit back and watch what feels like a car accident in slow motion. "Keep me posted."

As I'm leaving, Dillon asks, "Hey, you want to grab lunch today? Let's talk about what you have going on. I heard some weird rumor about one of your possible investments, and I wanted to talk to you a little bit about it."

"Sure. Anything to be concerned about?"

"I don't know. Let's figure this out together. Bring your file on Earth Path. We can have a quiet chat."

"Sure. What time you want to go?" I ask.

"Noon? We can head over to Scotty's Bar over by the Y. It's close enough to walk to, but we shouldn't have too many ears to eavesdrop," Dillon offers.

"I was there the other day. I actually ran into Annabelle there."

Mason gives me a funny look, and I don't want to get anyone in trouble, so I excuse myself and head back to my office to review a few more proposals and make some phone calls.

I meet up with Dillon at noon, and we walk the eight blocks over to Scotty's Bar and talk as we go. "I'm hearing that your Earth Path has their partnership fracturing and on the brink of splitting, which may affect us if we invest."

"The partners are splitting up? How did you hear that? I've not been told that yet."

"I heard it through a friend of a friend, so we want to make sure that we vet that information really carefully. I don't want to dump a few million in, and they split that money among themselves and leave us with no company."

I nod vigorously. "Agreed."

Over lunch, we go through my file on Earth Path, and we talk a little bit about Black Rock and my presentation on Sunday night.

"Any fun plans for the weekend?" Dillon asks as we walk back to the office.

"I suspect it'll be a quiet weekend. I started dating someone, and she's a grad student at Berkeley and needs to study and work this weekend."

"It looks like Cameron can't join us to play golf this weekend. Any interest in joining Mason, Trey, and me for golf on Saturday morning? We'll play down in Palo Alto?"

"I'd love to play. That would be great. I'll check with my girlfriend and make sure I'm correct about her plans."

"Just let me know. Emerson is happy to come, but I think she's looking for some girl time with her friends."

"I know we are doing a family thing on Saturday night, and I might bring her to the Arnaults' on Sunday night."

"I look forward to meeting her, but prepare her for the quiz from the girls. They'll put her through her paces in looking out for you."

"I don't think I'm worried about that. I'm more worried about what they might say about me."

He laughs loud and deep. "You'll be in good shape. They'll take good care of you."

When I return to my office, I see I missed a text from Bella while we walked back.

Bella: How are you feeling post-run today? Are your knuckles dragging on the ground yet?

Me: No, not yet. Actually, it is pretty invigorating. I think I need to do that more often. Although, it was a kick in the pants to get up so early.

Bella: I know it is, but it really helps me deal with some of the stress.

Me: I'm glad you got me out, and I commit to doing it again the next time. Speaking of which, what's your plan today?

Bella: I'm on BART now. Just left Berkeley. I'm headed over to the lab, and I'll work there probably pretty late. I didn't tell you this, but my lab manager quit last week.

Me: Oh crap, but are you telling me as your boyfriend or are you telling me as your potential investor?

Bella: Well, certainly as my boyfriend. Although... is that what we are calling ourselves?

Me: I think we can be safe to say that I'm comfortable with that. Are you?

Bella: Okay. I think so.

Me: Me too.

Bella: Then, as our potential investor, I'm telling you that we are looking for a new lab manager. I'm unclear on why the current lab manager left. One of my goals is to reach out to him and get some feedback so that when we hire a new replacement that we are able to fix what is wrong so that the next person doesn't leave.

Me: Great answer.

Me: I've been invited to play golf on Saturday morning, probably somewhat early, with some people from work. Are you okay with that?

Bella: Yes, absolutely. Don't let me hinder you. I have plenty of things to do this weekend, which will include hitting the farmers market before I head over to the lab and probably spend most of the day in the lab.

Me: We do have plans for your cousin's party on Saturday night. Let me know if I need to rent a tux or something.

Bella: You're funny. My family is not that formal. Dress like you did the day you came to my office.

Me: I know on Sunday you'll want to work, but I thought since I'm meeting your family on Saturday night, I will drag you to a dinner on Sunday night with the partners and significant others. How does that sound?

She's quiet, and I'm getting nervous. It takes some time before she responds.

Bella: Sorry, I was walking from BART to Muni. Sunday night sounds fun. I look forward to seeing you with your friends.

Me: You know, as long as you're there, I don't care what we're doing.

Bella: Have a great day. I'm just arriving at the lab. I'll text you when I'm headed home. Let me know if you want me to meet you. Did you like staying in the Mission last night?

Me: I will stay in the Mission as often as you let me. Have a great day.

I sit back in my chair, and savor this feeling. I'm totally excited about how this relationship is developing. Everything about her pleases me, and I can't believe how comfortable I feel with her so quickly.

chapter

FIFTEEN

ISABELLA

Walking into the lab, I'm stunned at how quiet it is for a midday afternoon. Turning to the receptionist, I ask, "Where is Dr. Johnson?"

"I'm not sure. He came in this morning and said he'd be back but didn't specify a time."

Part of me is really happy he's not here. The lab is active with the various scientists working on their roles, and everyone seems to have more spring in their step and be overall much happier without Dr. Johnson's presence. I need to figure out how to balance him better. Honestly, if we didn't need his technique on a new delivery system, which in our case would distribute the medication to the brain, I'd get rid of him.

Eventually, the scientists will be heading up teams, but right now they are doing all the grunt work and generating the data to support the efficacy of our studies. Currently, we are testing on particular plants and human brains of Parkinson patients who have died and donated their brains for a cure. We need to evaluate the disease and how the cells in the brain react. I walk through the recent experiments and look over the data. We are almost to the point where we can start some trials. And we hope that within a years' time, we are ready to do clinical trials. It's an ambitious schedule, but I've been working on this by myself for six years as a grad student, so we have a lot of research to fall back on.

Before Dr. Johnson returns, I decide I'm going to make the difficult call to Jim Thompson, our former lab manager, and determine why he left so suddenly. As I think about the recent turnover, I'm left wondering if Dr. Johnson is trying to get everyone to quit. It costs us time and money to hire replacements. I shake my head in disappointment. I dial and get my former lab manager's voice mail. "Hey, Jim. This is Isabella Vargas. What happened? Can you give me a callback? I understand if you don't want to come back and work for us anymore, but I'd like to understand what made you decide to quit so suddenly. You've been with me since the very beginning, and it's important to me that I understand. If we're doing something wrong, I'd like to fix it. I'd appreciate it if you could give me a call." I leave my personal cell phone number.

When I hang up, I hear Dr. Johnson yelling at one of our research scientists, and I walk out to see what's going on. "What's the problem?"

"I've got this," he informs me.

Tina looks like she's on the verge of tears.

"Tina, can you excuse us?" I say quietly.

She nods and runs out of the lab.

"You have no right to dismiss her like that."

"What could she have done that deserved a berating like you were giving her?"

"She's behind, and if she doesn't speed it up, I'm going to fire her."

"She probably wouldn't be behind if we still had a lab manager." I need to change the subject because I'm not going to let him fire her. "Where were you this morning?"

"Why does it matter?"

"Because I asked."

"I was looking at some possible new office and lab space."

"Why would you be looking at new space? We are eight months into a ten-year lease."

"You fucked up when you signed that lease. This space is going to be too small when we get this funding. We're going to need to add not only the lab portion but also set up for clinical studies. Plus we need to include space for marketing and sales and all kinds of different people to make sure that this becomes a possibility."

"We have more than enough room in this space. Marketing and sales won't be an issue until we've gone through multiple clinical trials and we are dealing with the FDA on trying to get approved. What happens if we are sold? There are so many opportunities and chances of things going sideways. To get this to market, we'll need over two-hundred million dollars. Why would we spend any venture capital on deadweight at this point? There's nothing for a marketing and sales team to do except be in the way and spend money we can use for development and research."

"You don't know how any of this works," he mocks. "Don't worry your little head about it. I got this all under control. You just worry about your part, and I'll worry about mine."

I try to control my anger. "You don't understand, Dr. Johnson, this is my part." I wave my hands around. "This is all my part. I hate to remind you, yet again, that I own 51 percent of this company. You have no ability to sign a contract with anyone without my approval."

He looks at me with death-ray eyes and then storms off. I swear I hear him say, "We'll just see about that."

I can't imagine that Christopher and SHN would agree with him. Why spend their money before we need to? There's just something that isn't right, and I can't quite figure out what it is.

My phone rings and distracts me. It's one of our suppliers.

"Ms. Vargas, we have a bill for just over eight thousand dollars that is over one hundred and twenty days overdue. We were wondering when you plan on paying the bill. We've also received an order from one of your scientists, but until we receive payment, we will not be able to fulfill the order."

"I'm sorry. This is news to me. I will check with our accounts payable and find what's happening."

"Thank you, Ms. Vargas. If we don't receive payment in five days, we will hand this over to collections, and you'll be unable to order from our supply house in the future without establishing a significant retainer."

"I see on my caller ID your number." I repeat it back to her. "Can I investigate and call you back?"

"Of course. Five days, Ms. Vargas," she stresses to me.

What the fuck? We have plenty of money in the bank.

I walk over to Mindy. "I just received a call from Lab Suppliers, and they tell me we're three months overdue on paying our bill. They are about to shut us off. Are you getting copies of the bills?"

She nods. "I've written checks and given them to Dr. Johnson, but he won't sign them."

"Do you know why?"

"He said we needed to show investors that we have money."

"What else is outstanding?"

"Every bill, with the exception of payroll. He told me once we get the funding, I can pay the vendors."

• • •

"That's a problem because we won't be seeing any money from the venture capital firm for six to eight months, and that's *if* they choose to invest in us. We're not expecting a check tomorrow or even next week. It'll be a while. How many bills do we have outstanding?"

"As I said, it's almost all of them."

"Can you put together a list of bills and our bank balance?"

"I have it put together already." She types a few keys on her keyboard, and I hear a document being printed. She hands it to me. My palms begin to sweat, and my stomach falls. I feel like I'm going to vomit. We only have enough money to become current and probably go another six months. How did we get so far off our budget? In our original business plan we could make it another two years before being desperate for cash.

"Please write checks for all of these outstanding bills and bring them to me for signature."

I take the list of bills and march into Dr. Johnson's office. He's on the phone on what sounds like a personal call with his investment advisor, but I don't care. He can talk to me now. He points to the door, and I cross my arms in defiance and then point to the spreadsheet.

He rolls his eyes and tells the person he's talking to, "I'll have to call you back. Yes, you can buy those stocks." He ends the call and turns back to me. "That was very rude."

"Well, I guess, like everyone else, you should take care of your personal business on your own time." He hates me, but I don't care. I hand him the printout that Mindy gave me.

"What is this?" he demands.

"This is a list of all our outstanding bills. We are about to be evicted, we are going to lose our laboratory supply house, and we are most likely going to have our lab equipment repossessed."

"That will never happen. They threaten, but that's all they'll do."

"We should have discussed this."

"I have my responsibilities, and this is one of them."

Breathing through my nose in staccato bursts to control the urge to reach across and punch him in the nose. "This is unacceptable."

"We'll get the check from SHN in the next few weeks, and we'll pay everyone."

"Christopher Reinhardt told me that they were a good six to eight months out from fully vetting us and writing us a check. Why would we hold bills for that long? We're in serious trouble if we are not paying our bills."

"You don't understand how to manage a business."

"Maybe not, but I know that we want people to pay us timely, so we pay timely."

When I turn to leave, he yells after me, "If you take money out of our checking account, we won't get the funding."

"I imagine that having several creditors chasing us down for money would be a bigger concern for them."

"I told you I'm the one worrying about all of this. You need to just concentrate on your side while I concentrate on mine."

I put my finger in his weasel face, so there is no question as to my seriousness. "What you don't understand is that since I own 51 percent of this company, I'm financially responsible for 51 percent of the debt, and if this goes under because of your financial malfeasance, then we have a bigger problem. I'm going to owe money on your crap, and *that* is unacceptable."

"No need to get bitchy with me just because it's your time of the month."

I stop in my tracks. There is no way he just referred to my menstrual cycle. I look to the ceiling and clinch my fists at my side. I consider slapping him, kicking him in his tiny balls, or just flat out firing him. In as menacing voice as I can muster, I tell him, "Your comment is completely inappropriate. I'll be signing all checks today. You need to figure out what's going on and where your priorities are, and this company better be a priority."

• • •

"A priority for me? I'm not the one who comes in here three days a week after one o'clock in the afternoon."

"Yes, you're right, you don't come in at one o'clock in the afternoon, but I also don't see you here at two o'clock in the morning closing down."

"I don't take orders from you."

That's as good as he can dish. I know I've already won, and my blood pressure goes down significantly. "Actually, Dr. Johnson, you do take orders from me as long as I own the majority share of this business. Check your contract." I march out of his office and into my own. I'm so angry with him I can't see straight.

I text Christopher.

Me: Can you meet me for coffee right now?

Christopher: In a half hour?

Me: That's fine. I'll come to you.

Christopher: There's a Starbucks across the street from our building.

Me: See you in a half hour.

I look up as Mindy places several checks in front of me. I scoop them up, thanking her. "I'll be delivering these to the post office myself."

"I've worked for several start-ups, and in my experience, Dr. Johnson isn't correct," Mindy whispers at me.

I look around, and just above a whisper, I say, "Thanks, Mindy. I hate to put you in an awkward situation, but let me know if he does anything shifty this afternoon while I'm out."

"No problem."

• • •

My rideshare drops me at Starbucks. I'm early, but I order drinks for both of us and sit at a table and begin signing the checks. These are going to hurt. We won't have a lot in our checking account to make it six months. I'm not sure where I'm going to find the funding to cover us until we do get the money—if we get the money.

Christopher comes in and kisses me on the cheek. "Hi, what a pleasant surprise."

I smile at him and try to put my argument with my business partner aside. "I'm glad you could make it work."

"What happened? I can see something has upset you."

"I want to ask my boyfriend a question and not my potential investor. Can you do that for me?"

He nods slowly.

I open the file and show him what I found and that I'm paying the bills. "Is he right? Do you want to see that we've got money?"

"You're both right. We do want to see you have money in the bank, but it would be a bigger concern if you are in collections on your debt."

I never cry, but that is all I want to do right now as I feel my dream of finding a new medication for Parkinson's so close but quickly becoming out of reach. "The interest we accrued on these bills make up a month of our operating budget." I look at him with tears pooling in my eyes. "We'll never make six months. I've drained everything I have ever had and leveraged my mother's house."

"As your boyfriend, I will tell you let's see what we can figure out." He reaches for my hand and squeezes it. "Can you stay with me tonight?"

We drink our coffee, and he tells me a story of what is going on with one of the partners in his firm who is dealing with the Russian mob. I try to pay attention, but I'm only half listening. I'm moving from angry to scared.

"Do you want to come upstairs and meet some of the team?"

I stand on my tiptoes and kiss him on the cheek. "I'd better not. I have a ton of work to get done."

"Okay, but promise me to call when you're heading home, and I'll come over."

When I return to the office, Mindy informs me that Dr. Johnson left shortly after I did. "Thanks," I tell her.

I try to work through the data flowing in from six scientists and do the lab manager's job and my own. My mind keeps wandering to what Dr. Johnson could be up to. I'm not concentrating and finally give up about ten o'clock. It's a short day for me, but I can't do any more. I'm exhausted, and I'm still quite angry. I'm not getting much work done, and I keep dwelling on how I want to shred him a new one.

As I ride home in the rideshare, I think about Christopher. He's smart, God knows he's absolutely gorgeous, he's great in bed, he's totally into me, and I'd be a fool if I didn't explore this further. But I'm not sure that the timing is right for us. I decide I can't see him tonight.

Me: Heading home. Exhausted and going to bed early. Let's talk tomorrow.

Christopher: I'm disappointed, but I understand. We'll figure something out. Do you want to try to escape for lunch tomorrow—isn't it your day in the lab all day?

Me: No, I better not. Things are kind of crazy right now with the loss of the lab manager. And I need to figure out some things.

Christopher: We're still on for Saturday's party, right?

Could my cousin's party be at any worse time? Crap.

Me: Are you crazy? Of course! There's no way that we could get out of it at this point. My family is preparing questionnaires for you to answer. Don't be alarmed if somebody brings out a group list of questions to ask you.

Christopher: LOL that would be funny. We could write a book on how to integrate yourself into your family.

Me: There's no other family like mine. It would scare all men like *Fatal Attraction* did in the 80s. Have a good night. Sleep well.

Christopher: Sleep well. Let me know if you change your mind about lunch. We'll handle your challenges at Black Rock together.

My week continues to not add up. I'm doing the job of the lab manager and seemingly taking care of everything else around the lab, but I'm not sure exactly where to find Dr. Johnson.

I've spoken to Christopher every night this week, and I know he's wanted to be with me, but he can be a distraction. Teaching three mornings a week and being present for my students, being a leader in the lab, and working until at least midnight, but often later, has my stress levels high. Last night during our conversation, Christopher talked me into spending the weekend together. He assures me I'll have plenty of time to work, and I hope he's right. We'll split our time between his place and mine, and we'll go to my family event, and I'll go to his work dinner on Sunday night.

My overnight bag is packed, and I've committed to meeting him at his place by six. My cell phone pings.

Christopher: It's 6:05. Are you still sitting at your desk?

I smile. He knows me so well.

Me: I'm just shutting down.

Christopher: I'm waiting out front. Hurry, we have dinner reservations.

I'm turning lights off and set the alarm.

True to his word, his car is sitting outside the front door. As I'm in the car, he pulls me in for a kiss, and I taste the mint and smell his woodsy scent.

"I've missed you this week," he confides.

"Thank you for making me do this."

"I can't make you do anything. But I promise you can work a good part of the weekend, and I'll try to keep my hands to myself." I look at him confused, and he grins. "At least while you're working."

I chuckle. "That's all I'm looking for."

"We have a dinner reservation at seven. You look just fine for where we're going, but if you want to go back to my place and change or whatever, let me know."

"Normally, I'd want to go and take a shower, so my boyfriend always thinks I smell like roses." I lift my arms and smell my pits to add some levity. "But I figure I'm okay for dinner."

"You're always okay." He reaches for my hand, holding it as he drives us across town. My heart flutters. I'm really beginning to like this guy.

He pulls into a parking space, and we walk the half block to the restaurant. When we walk in, it's like we're transformed into what I imagine Tuscany looks like. The walls have hand-painted murals in muted colors of vineyards and a stunning old castle at sunset. The smell of garlic, tomatoes, and freshly baked bread make my stomach growl. I'm starving.

They put us in a quiet corner, and we sit close to one another, the chemistry sparkling between us. I want so much to take him while he's sitting next to me—public place be damned!

"Christopher, what are you doing here?" A woman walks up to the table, and immediately I'm jealous. She greets him with a hug and kiss. I instantly dislike her. She's beautiful with almost jet-black hair, stunning blue eyes, and she's petite. Where is this big, green-eyed, ugly monster coming from?

Then I notice the giant rock on her left hand as Christopher turns to me and says, "Bella, this is Greer Ford. She works with me at SHN." Turning to Greer, he says, "Greer, this is my girlfriend, Isabella Vargas."

She lights up and completely ignores Christopher. "I'm absolutely thrilled to meet you. I wish I could say Christopher has told us all about you, but he's so private."

"Well, it's rather new," I explain.

Turning to Christopher, she asks, "When are you bringing her to a Sunday night dinner?" She turns to me and explains, "All the partners get together on Sunday evenings for a partners' meeting. We gather first for dinner, and we often bring our significant others. I promise we're very kind." She winks at me, and the green-eyed monster of jealousy dissolves completely. I like her.

"She'll be there Sunday night," Christopher promises.

"I'm a doctoral candidate at Berkeley, and I'm in a crunch for time," I explain.

"We'll have lots of questions for you, but I promise we are very nice." A gentleman comes over and hands her a bag. "Grazie, Filippo. Make sure you take good care of my friends tonight, but if they give you any trouble, you let me know, and I'll make their lives miserable." She smiles at Christopher, and we know she's just teasing.

"You tell that man of yours that I need more wine," Filippo says in a thick Italian accent.

"I promise." They kiss on both cheeks. Turning to us, she says, "Filippo will take excellent care of you. I can't wait to see you on Sunday." And in a whirl, she waves and is out the door.

"Sorry about that." Christopher blushes.

"Actually, I'm glad I got to meet her. It'll make Sunday night a little easier walking into the wolf's den. Does her fiancé sell wine?"

"You could say that. He's the one who owns Bellisima Vineyards up in Napa."

"Wow. Didn't they just win a huge award?"

"They did. They won the Decanter Platinum award. We're worried she's going to go to work for the family vineyard and leave us. She runs all of our public relations and is a real dynamo. Her works helps make us successful." He cuddles in close, and says, "Enough talk about my coworker. Tell me about your week? Did Dr. Johnson resurface?"

We settle in to a nice conversation and enjoy ourselves.

"So, when are you going to tell me what I need to know for tomorrow night?"

"I've never taken anyone to a family event, so I don't know what to tell you." I try to imagine going to my aunt's house and what he can expect. "It'll be all family: aunts, uncles, cousins, some kids, some girlfriends and boyfriends. It's really a backyard family event and the food will be good, but, be prepared, it'll be spicy."

"I'll bring some Tums. Your mom will be there?"

"Yes, but not my dad. He's in a facility for Parkinson's. He does okay for a few hours in the morning, but by lunch he's already sunset and the change in scenery is really hard on him."

"That must be tough."

"He has a tremendous shake and talks incredibly slow, but as long as I visit him in the morning, we're okay."

"I'm ready for your mom."

I snort. "You could never be ready for her. She is the woman who drove me harder than I drove myself. She's incredibly hard to please and really has no filter. Just be aware."

"I told you, I'm ready."

When we've finished dinner, we hold hands and walk casually back to Christopher's car. I'm shocked when I see the broken glass on the sidewalk. I don't remember walking around it when we went into the restaurant, and then I look up and see the damage to his car. I panic. My computer, my research, and my notes for my class on Monday were in the car. I gasp in horror.

We rush to examine the car. My computer is missing but not my bag. I want to cry. I hear Christopher on the phone, "Yes, I'd like to report vandalism and theft to my car." He gives them our location and assures them, "Yes, we'll be here waiting."

Christopher holds me tight as I cry. I've backed things up on the cloud, so it isn't a disaster, but I can't afford a new computer right now with everything going on. The police come and take our statements. As I watch them fingerprint his car, I experience a strange mixture of being numb and feeling violated.

When the police leave, we drive back to his place. It's cold without the window. "I'm grateful to have a garage tonight."

I nod.

"I've got a plan, and this isn't going to affect you for very long. I promise."

He doesn't understand that without a computer, I'm screwed. I take my overnight bag, and we head up to his place. We aren't inside but a few moments when the buzzer to the front door rings, and I almost jump out of my skin.

He allows the person in and goes to meet them at the door while I head to the bathroom. I need to take a shower and wash away this terrible week. Maybe someone is trying to tell me that I need to make some changes in my life. Black Rock's research is pivotal to getting my PhD. Maybe I should redirect myself to medical school like my mother says or maybe just work as a scientist within another therapeutic start-up. I start to cry big ugly tears. Why can't things go right?

I hear the shower door behind me, and then his arms slide around me. Tension radiates from my body. I press my face into his chest, my hands against his biceps.

"Shh, I promise, it's all going to be okay," he tries soothing me.

I hold on to him and cry harder. He kisses me on my head and holds me tighter, and I feel his erection pulsating just above my sweet spot. I want to forget tonight and just enjoy my time with him. Lifting my head, I kiss him, hard and feral.

I ease closer, skimming my breasts against his bare chest, skin to skin, warmth to warmth, the way I want it to be. The shower is sensual. He washes my hair and body, taking time to caress me as he goes. When he's done, I'm ready for anything, having forgotten all about my week.

After toweling me dry, he leads me to the bedroom. "Bella." His voice is rough and thick with emotion. He tangles his fingers in my damp hair and tips my face up before sliding his lips over mine until I ache with the need to have him closer. His tongue delves into my mouth, hot and wet, as he pulls me backward toward the bed. My legs bump the mattress, and he gently lifts me onto the large bed, his mouth never leaving mine. His hands graze my bare skin to knead and mold my breasts.

Heat races through my veins, pooling in my stomach, trickling down between my legs. But it isn't that mind-numbing desire I've felt before. It is richer, a stronger need than I've ever felt—not just for sex or a release but for him.

He rolls and pulls me on top of him. "You're so beautiful," he rasps.

I love the sound of his voice, the way he says his compliments—not to get into my pants, but because he believes it. I arch into him, needing to feel every part of his body against mine.

His hand snakes out over the side of the bed, and I know he's reaching for his pants to find his wallet. Pulling out a condom, he rips the foiled packet and offers me the condom. His hard cock takes my breath away as I roll it on him.

He runs a hand down my cheek in a barely there caress. "God, you make me feel whole when I didn't know I was broken before."

Those mesmerizing eyes of his streak over my naked body as he moves his hands to skim and explore my curves with the slightest touch. He lifts his head to press his lips to the base of my throat, and I shudder at the warm sensation. One of his big hands settles at my waist as the fingers of his other hand dip into my burning wetness. I moan and curve against his probing fingers, against his thumb, circling and teasing.

The hot tip of his erection brushes my center, almost home, and with that one touch, anticipation blooms into full-blown desire to have him hard and deep. His breath catches when I shiver and rub against his arousal, sending just enough pressure to my core to make me light-headed. He sweeps his hands up my ribs to cup my breasts. "Go slow. I want to remember every inch sliding inside you."

If the look in his eyes hasn't nearly stopped my heart, his husky words do. Forget falling for him. I already have. "Kiss me, Christopher."

He lifts his head and slides his tongue into my mouth just as I lower myself and claim him with my body. Our joining is slow and slick, heated rod against clenching glove. I pull him tight, tighter, until long moments later he is buried to the hilt.

I sigh into his mouth, loving his hard length deep inside, knowing I can never tire of the way he makes me feel. "Love me, Bella." My heart kicks over. I'm afraid I'm headed in that direction. I know I'm probably not going to be able to stop it.

I slowly rock my hips, which brings a groan from him and a tightening to his hands as they dart over my back and pull me closer. I fear it can't last, but I want to draw out the moment, to memorize every sound and sensation and the smoldering look in his dark eyes as I ride him.

He thrusts upward at my rocking, and my pleasure builds until I can't fight it anymore. I grip tighter with my muscles, pulling him closer to the edge, wanting to feel him go over with me. And when he does, when I feel that deep pulse of his release, my orgasm explodes through every limb in my body, shooting me down a slippery slope and into an abyss, and I know there's no way out for me.

The alarm goes off, and it's still dark outside. He holds me tight and kisses the top of my head, before saying, "I'll be right back."

He returns a few minutes later. "I had this delivered last night." He presents a box with the latest computer model pictured on the white box. I must look confused. He begins unpacking it. "I know there's no way you can work and finish your studies without a computer."

"But I can't afford this." Just looking at the box, I can tell it's worth more than I make in two months. "Particularly this computer."

He smiles at me. "But I can, and I don't mind. Let me do this for you. It's my fault for not taking your computer inside with us or running it here last night."

"It's not your fault," I implore. I'm relieved that I have a computer. I'll reimburse him one day because I know that I also bear part of the burden because I didn't even think about my computer in the back seat of his car.

"My insurance will pick up most of this, so don't worry about it. We'll need to upload the software you need on it, but it should have the basics already, so it should be easy. We can use my credit card, and I'll just send it off to the insurance company."

He plugs in the new computer, and it fires up. It's so much faster than what I'm used to. Kissing me on the forehead, he says, "I'll make us some breakfast. Start making a list of what you need to download, and let's get that done this morning."

I'm exploring the new computer when he walks in with a steaming plate of eggs, bacon, and toast. "Eat something."

I take two bites and put the plate down, focusing on what I need to do. A black American Express card is pushed under my nose. "Order whatever you need."

"I feel really bad taking advantage of you, Christopher."

"You're not taking advantage of me. As I said, I'm just going to submit it all to the insurance company." I reluctantly take the card from him. "Dillon will be here in a few minutes. You have all morning to yourself. I should be back by one. Does that work for you?"

I nod. I have so much to consider that I'm not sure where I should start.

I work like crazy downloading and pulling the research off my cloud server. I don't think I lost anything too drastic. I change all the passwords on the cloud, despite figuring that whoever stole my computer has most likely wiped the memory and sold it to some poor student in desperate need of a computer.

Time flies, and the next thing I know, Christopher has returned. He smells of sweat and tastes of salt and beer. "Did you have any problems getting what you need?"

I hand him back his credit card. "Not at all, and thankfully almost everything was on the cloud, so I didn't lose much."

He kisses me on my forehead. I feel a level of comfort I've never felt before. "I'm going to take a shower. What time do we need to leave for your aunt's?"

"There will be a dinner, and the party will commence afterward. Maybe five- thirty?"

"Okay, I have an appointment to get the car window replaced. It should be done long before we need to leave."

I don't see him for the afternoon. When I start to get ready for the evening, despite the time it took to get everything lined up, I realize I was able to get a lot of things completed, and I don't feel behind. Maybe dating Christopher is something I can do right now.

chapter

SIXTEEN

CHRISTOPHER

The party is in her aunt's backyard, and there are people everywhere. I'm introduced to easily thirty cousins and many of their spouses, girlfriends, or boyfriends. It's almost overwhelming.

"I hope I won't have a test on all their names later," I mutter into Bella's hair as I kiss her.

"I know it's a lot, don't worry. The only important one is my mother." She grabs me by the hand and leads me to the kitchen. "Mama? Can you take a small break and meet Christopher?"

I see a small woman who looks like an older version of Bella wipe wet hands on an apron tied around her waist. "I'm trying to keep up with the dishes." She extends her hand. "It's wonderful to meet you, Christopher."

"So nice to meet you, Dr. Vargas. I can see the similarities between you and Isabella."

She smiles proudly. "There is a lot of her father hidden in there too."

"I look forward to meeting him someday." Her smile become restrained, and I hope she isn't upset that I referenced her husband.

"Mama, don't spend the whole party here in the kitchen. Come outside and visit with us," Bella beckons.

"Let me finish a few things, and I'll come out to you," she assures us.

We get in line for a plate of food. Many of the old aunts come up and flirt with me, and the men size me up. Bella rolls her eyes. "They think you look like a movie star."

"Wow, that's quite the compliment." I smile at her.

"It's the sapphire blue eyes."

Dinner is an amazing spread of various Mexican dishes. I load up my plate, and we sit at a table. I'm about halfway through the meal when Bella's mother sits down. "I appreciate you taking such good care of my daughter."

"I'm happy to do so," I tell her.

"Are you going to fund her company?"

I put my fork down so I can address her obvious concern. "It's not up to me. In my company, it has to pass through multiple groups for approval."

"Do you know why this research means so much to her?"

I nod. "I believe it's because her father has Parkinson's."

"Good, so you understand." I can tell she doesn't trust me. She probably thinks I'm only after her for sex, but I'll show her that I want something more.

"Mama, he knows all about Papa. He's looked through my research. It'll take some time."

Turning to her daughter, she asks, "What will happen to you when he decides to not fund your start-up?"

"I'll figure something out, Mama. This research is too important."

"You can go to medical school and treat neurological patients."

I see Bella close her eyes. "Mama, getting a PhD isn't a bad thing."

"Academia is not enough. You'll be eaten alive."

"Hopefully my company sees her research and finances Black Rock," I interject before World War III breaks out.

"Don't give her false hope, Christopher. She needs a backup plan, and you aren't it."

"I don't think I am her backup plan. I think your daughter is bright, inventive, curious, and has an innate ability to figure out problems. I think research is perfect for her, and if she wants to teach, she can fall back on that."

"You're foolish to think that, Christopher. She needs people in her life that are honest with her. Not just wanting to get into her pants."

"Mama! You need to apologize to Christopher," Bella demands.

I hold my hand up. "No, she doesn't, Bella. She knows I'm only trying to be supportive, and I know she's looking out for you."

I finally think I've broken through. Her lips curl. "You're a smart one, aren't you, Christopher?"

"Well, I went to medical school myself, and I know that practicing medicine isn't for everyone."

Her eyes go wide, and then she smiles at me. "No, it isn't, but I'm glad you understand the pressures on my baby girl."

"I do, and I try hard to make sure I'm not one of them."

She nods and gets up, and as she leaves she says, "Make sure you say goodbye to your aunts before you leave."

Bella turns to me. "I'm sorry about that."

"It wasn't anything I didn't expect. But remember this when you meet my family. They have expectations of me that I didn't meet either."

We dance for a while. When there's a slow song, I pull Bella into me and hold her close. I know there are many eyes on us, so I'm careful where my hands are and what we do. I see her oldest aunt walk up and tap Bella on the shoulder. "I'd like to cut in."

Bella looks at me questioning. I nod, and her aunt steps in. "You're very handsome, you know."

I don't know what to say. How do you respond when a woman who could be your mother talks about your looks? "Thank you."

"I hear you're rich too."

I'm a little taken aback by her forthrightness. "Really? Who told you that?"

"I saw the car you drove up in, and I see your watch. I notice things," she says triumphantly.

I laugh loudly. "Well, don't believe everything you see."

"I like a man who's modest. If you give up on our Bella, give me a call." She pinches my ass and winks at me.

I grin widely. "I have no plans on giving up on your Bella."

As the song ends, she whispers in my ear, "I've told everyone you're very good for our Bella. Don't make a liar out of me."

"I'll try."

She kisses me on the cheek.

"What did you two talk about?" Bella inquires.

"You mostly. All good, I promise."

"Do tell."

"Nothing to tell, really."

We say our goodbyes to everyone and head out to the car.

"You were a great sport tonight," Bella coos.

"It was fun. Thank you for inviting me."

We get in the car, and we aren't even to the interstate when I look over and see she's napping. I don't mind. She works hard and needs her rest.

When we arrive at her place, I jostle Bella. "Hey, sleepyhead, wake up. We're at your place."

She looks around with her eyes wide. "I'm so sorry. I didn't mean to fall asleep."

"You're tired. Don't worry about it."

We walk into her apartment, and she's a little lost. I point her to her sleep shorts and a camisole, and I tuck her into bed. I step out of my pants, leaving my boxers on, and crawl in behind her, and she spoons with me. It's been a long day, and I drift off quickly.

I wake early and reach for her, but the bed is cold. Sitting up, I look across the room and see her bent over with her pencil in her mouth, studying her computer screen.

"Hey, have you been up long?"

Looking at the clock, she says, "Just a couple hours. I have a lot to get done today before we go to dinner tonight."

"Can I go get you a cup of coffee, or would you want to come with me to get it? I was going to hit that hipster coffee spot on Mission Street."

"I suppose I could take a break in a little bit and go with you."

I like that idea, so I shower and get dressed and start preparing for my day. I really need to give her her space; plus I need to prepare myself for tonight's dinner. I set myself up in the kitchen to work on my presentation, but I need coffee and some sort of sustenance.

"Are you at a point you can take a break?"

She's dressed in yoga pants and one of my Carolina T-shirts. "Where did you get that?"

"I might have liberated it from your closet to remind me of you when you aren't around."

My chest puffs out further, and her comment makes me really happy. "It looks good on you."

We wander the street to a little Italian coffee spot. I call it a hipster place because the coffee is expensive and the patrons are way cooler than I am. We order pastries and large cups of Illy coffee, enjoying a little bit of morning together while reading through the newspapers. She reads the *San Francisco Chronicle,* and I read the *New York Times* and the *Wall Street Journal*.

Life is incredibly comfortable together, and I feel like I can do this for a very long time. We walk back to her place holding hands.

"I'm really sorry about my mother and my aunt last night."

"You've nothing to be sorry about. Just wait until you meet my family. You'll be equally tortured."

She spends the day crawling through her computer and the data that she's received from some of the scientists in her lab. I work through my presentation and watch a hockey game. When we are about an hour and a half from leaving, I let her know so she can prepare. I've learned that if I start giving her time alerts, she seems to be able to wrap things up and is less stressed.

"Okay, I'll be ready."

She takes a shower, and then I hear the hair dryer going. I just sit patiently on the couch. She changes in to a pair of jeans that make me appreciate her backside and a tight sweater that shows off her curves. The guys can eat their hearts out. She grabs an overnight bag and throws it in the back of my car along with her messenger bag. As we drive down to Hillsboro to our dinner and meeting, we talk about what she can expect. I don't want to sway her opinion of anyone, so I'm careful to just give her the highlights.

I pull into the circular driveway amongst many other cars and turn to her. "There's going to be a pack of dogs any second that will come barreling out of the house and surround the car to greet you. Are you afraid of dogs? I've never asked that before. They're just curious when everyone arrives."

"No, I'm good with dogs. I grew up with several."

No sooner than the car turns off, we're surrounded by half a dozen dogs in various sizes, barking and greeting us. I get out on my side and walk over and shoo them away before opening Bella's door for her. As she exits the car, I can see she's a little nervous. I kiss her temple. "You're going to do great."

She grabs her messenger bag, and I grab mine, and we walk in the house while the dogs are distracted by the next car arriving. The first person we meet is Margo, and I introduced her. "Bella, this is Margo, and this is her house. Margo, this is Bella, my girlfriend."

Margo opens her arms, brings Bella into a hug, and says, "We're so happy to meet you. It's nice to see someone has finally captured Christopher's heart."

"Thank you, it's great to meet you."

Greer rushes over and hugs Bella with several of the women trailing behind her. I know she's shared meeting her already with the girls.

"Isabella, it's so wonderful that you came," Greer gushes.

"Please call me Bella."

"Of course. Bella, I'd like you to meet CeCe. She's one of our advisers, as is her father, and this is her parents' home."

"Nice to meet you." Bella says.

"Give me a hug. You've tamed the man I didn't think could ever be tamed." CeCe demands with a huge grin.

Bella looks at me carefully. "Did he date a lot?"

"We've never met anyone. We knew he dated, but he's never brought anyone here. We're so glad."

Greer continues, "This is Sara. She's our chief legal counsel and happens to be CeCe's sister-in-law."

"So nice to meet you."

Sara squeezes her hand. "We're thrilled you're here."

"This beautiful redhead is Hadlee. She's engaged to Cameron, one of the partners."

"Don't let this group intimidate you. I've known many of them for a while and know all their weaknesses," Hadlee jokes.

"This blonde bombshell is Emerson," Greer says.

"I met you and Caroline at the farmers market a few weeks ago. At Jordana's, remember?" Bella shares.

"That's right," CeCe says. "My friends call me CeCe. You did my mother's flowers—which she absolutely loved."

"Oh my goodness, I remember that," Emerson adds. "You were with another woman who was just adorable."

"Yes, I was with my best friend, Ellie. It's great to see you again."

Greer looks pleased that Bella is already acquainted with some of her friends. She continues making introductions. "And this is Annabelle. She's involved with our managing partner, Mason."

"Nice to meet you," Bella murmurs.

"How did you two meet?" CeCe asks.

"Believe it or not, we met at The Church."

"A Catholic church or the new club in SOMA?" CeCe inquires.

"The club—although I should remember to call it a Catholic church, so my family digests it better." The group laughs. "I was at my best friend's birthday party, and he was chivalrous when someone wasn't taking a hint and going away. He pretended to be my boyfriend, and here we are."

"I like that chivalrous way about him," Emerson says.

Dillon walks over, puts his arm around Emerson's shoulders, and introduces himself. "Hi. I'm Dillon, and I work with Christopher here. I can tell you all the good, the bad, and the ugly."

I'm almost ready to protest when I spot the evil eye Emerson gives him. "That's not true. He's an honest golfer, and he saves damsels in distress. Run along and don't spoil this for him."

"I think we've been dismissed," Dillon says to me.

I look at Bella and raise my eyebrows to make sure she's comfortable with the girls. Her smile puts me at ease.

"I think we can pull together two foursomes if everyone wants to play," Cameron says.

"Are you in?" Mason looks at me expectantly.

"When are you talking about going?" I ask.

"Friday afternoon. Does Bella play?" he inquires.

"I don't think she plays, but she doesn't go out much. She's pretty wrapped up in Black Rock and finishing the research for her dissertation."

Margo calls dinner, stopping our golf outing plans, and we work our way to the dining room. Margo directs Bella on where she'd like us to sit. Looking around the room, I notice that it is getting full, but I think we could easily add another ten people if we needed to, and probably an additional six if they changed out the chairs. I don't know how much longer we'll be able to continue these dinners, but I enjoy them. The added bonus is that we include our significant others; I really value that the company puts focus on more than the heavy hours that we work.

Margo and her small army of helpers bring out several racks of lamb and places them throughout the table. They bring dishes of fingerling potatoes, grilled artichokes halves, salads, string beans, and sautéed mushrooms.

Bella looks at me. "Do you always eat like this?"

I nod, and CeCe says, "My mom loves to entertain. This is the highlight of her week."

Margo looks at her daughter with affection. "Yes, it is. The energy in the room is young and vibrant, and it's fun to plan the menus."

"Dinner is outstanding," Bella says. "Thank you for including me."

We laugh and joke through dinner, mostly to try to impress Bella. I'm really enjoying myself. Finally, Margo's team brings out strawberry rhubarb pie with vanilla ice cream for each of us.

• • •

When the grandfather clock on the wall rings eight o'clock, we—the partners and advisers—all retreat into Charles's office.

"You've chosen a nice girl," Charles offers.

"Thank you. I think so too," I tell him.

We go through our agenda, and I'm second on the list.

When it becomes my turn, I hand out a paper copy of a PowerPoint presentation, and I walk them through Black Rock Therapeutics and their needs. I explain that Bella is one of the founders at Black Rock and stress that I met her before my meetings started with Black Rock and didn't know her involvement until after I had spoken with Dr. Johnson on multiple occasions.

Emerson fidgets in her seat, and I know her well enough to know something is bothering her. I prepare myself for her to say I'm too close to this. Taking a steadying breath, I ask, "Emerson, you seem to have some questions?"

She picks her words carefully. "What are you recommending?"

That's the hard question to answer. I know a lot more through my relationship with Bella, and I don't trust Dr. Johnson. "I don't want to influence anyone, but I'd recommend that we move forward with Black Rock to the next round of evaluation. I think their technology and what they're trying to develop is, from my research, cutting edge and a very interesting replacement and possible improvement to Parkinson's care."

"How are they financially?" Dillon asks.

I sit back in my chair and carefully figure out how I'm going to answer this without destroying the credibility of my relationship with Bella. "It's going to be tight for them to wait six months for funding. They're getting close. They've probably got about two to three months of funding to cover rent, equipment leases, and payroll."

"Anyway for them to offset the cash crunch?" Mason asks.

"I'm not sure." I look at Dillon, and ask, "What do you think after looking at their books?

"There are a few things that seem a little strange, but it could easily be a bookkeeping issue. I can't say for sure without interviewing the person doing the accounting."

"What kind of relationship do Dr. Johnson and Bella have?" Sara asks.

"Well, it's a partnership. She owns 51 percent. Although I have to tell you, when I met with Dr. Johnson, he didn't represent himself as the minority owner but rather the sole owner. It may be because Bella doesn't have his credentials, but Bella set me straight the first time we met in their offices and has included their partnership agreement, which is attached at the back of your handout."

"Have you asked him why he misrepresented himself? In my experience, he may have something up his sleeve to take the company out from under her," Emerson advises.

"I haven't asked—not because I was afraid of his answer, but because under normal circumstances I wouldn't ask, and I didn't want it to appear I'm favoring my girlfriend."

Mason sits back in his chair. "What are some of your concerns?"

I weigh my options carefully. Finally, I share, "Well, part of my concerns come from my relationship with Bella. Dr. Johnson always positioned the company as his own. He occasionally referred to a research assistant, but she wasn't there the first time we met. I asked for a meeting, and he was slow to set it up, so I showed up unannounced, and it ended up being Bella. I only wanted to speak to the researcher because he couldn't answer my questions about the research. My second concern is that in his initial request, his proposal was ten million, but once we started meeting, he adjusted to fifty million. I don't have a great feeling as to why the investment requirement is so much steeper. He's the name to invest in, but I'm concerned if, as Emerson says, he takes the company out from under Bella, he won't be the guy to get it over the finish line."

Emerson says, "Thank you, Christopher."

"She described it as her job is the science side of the company and he's the business side. Quite honestly, I'm not sure where his business head is at because he's made some decisions businesswise that I'm not a hundred percent sure about. I've not looked at their books, and these are based on Bella's view rather than an actual business perception. And, with all of that being said, I would say that I believe that the business is a sound decision. There are competitors out there, and we all know that getting therapeutics to market requires a runway of about $300 million, so it's pretty significant to ask at this point for something at this stage. I also know that there are three pharma companies that might be interested in them, and it might be something we could offload quickly. So there are a lot of options."

"How close is Bella to getting her PhD?" Sara asks.

"This research is a major part of her dissertation, so I'd imagine a good year to eighteen months out," I tell her. I ask the question I know that Bella will want to know. "I guess the bigger question would be, can we do the investment without Bella or without Dr. Johnson?"

"Dr. Johnson's credentials and award make it a much better buy. So the reality is, we could do it without Bella but probably not Dr. Johnson."

I'm completely crushed. This is Bella's baby, and I know that she is the science behind this drug. I need to figure out how to get the two of them working together cohesively. "I can leave the room if you all would like to talk about this without me being present. I realize that, given my relationship with Bella, I'm compromised."

"I think you're fine," Charles says. "I'm okay with moving this to the next level, and then maybe we can have discussions about whether or not we move forward with Black Rock."

I nod. "I'll send over the NDA and see if I can't move this along." We hear the dogs going absolutely crazy and Margo yelling at them to come back inside as they're running in and out of the front door.

CeCe rolls her eyes. "It must be a raccoon."

We go through several other prospects, and an hour and a half later, we finally finish up. As we drive back into the city, Bella shares, "I really like the culture that your company has, particularly with your leadership team, and I really wish that was something we had over at Black Rock. It certainly is something I wouldn't mind exploring and trying to make happen with my team."

chapter

SEVENTEEN

ISABELLA

I really had a nice weekend with Christopher. Each time I look at him, I think of all the things I want to do to him and have him do to me. He's been a little distant since the partners' meeting, and I have a feeling they spent a lot of time talking about Black Rock because several mentioned it when they were done with their meeting; I'm cautiously optimistic they will fund us.

We decided we were going to stay at Christopher's, so when the alarm sounds early on Monday morning, we start our regular routine of going for a run. It's three and a half miles round trip that we pound our way through. I like the change in the scenery of our run.

After we shower and dress, Christopher drops me at Union Station so I can take BART into Berkeley, and he goes in to work. It's a nice routine.

After a long morning of teaching, I spend some time in the department, keeping my office hours, and I run into my advisor.

"How are things going at Black Rock?"

"I think we are hitting our stride. Would you like to look at some of our research data?"

"I'd love to." He pulls up a chair, and I walk him through the various data and show him some of our promising results.

"I'm impressed. You look like you might be on to something."

"I hope so."

"How are things going with Dr. Johnson?"

"We haven't found our groove yet, but I'm sure we will."

He looks at me funny and wishes me well as I pack up to get back to the lab in San Francisco.

I greet Mindy, and she smiles at me. As I start down to my office, I hear, "Ms. Vargas, I'd like to see you in my office."

"Of course." I drop my things off in my office and put my lab coat on, not sure what Dr. Johnson will want to see. Then I join him in his office.

"Why weren't you in the lab this weekend?"

I'm a bit startled by his question. "I wasn't physically in the lab this weekend, but I worked all weekend."

"Where are you with your research?"

I'm not sure where he's going with this, but I try to answer truthfully. "Well, I had a little bit of a hiccup on Friday night when my computer was stolen out of the back seat of my boyfriend's car, but everything is all good now. I was back up by Saturday morning and continued to go through the data all weekend."

"Why haven't you posted it on the server?"

I rarely post data to the server, particularly on weekends when I can never be sure our data won't be breached. "Because I haven't quite figured something else out and wanted to explore it with our lead scientist"

"Well, let's get a move on it; we're not here to play. I hate these days that you come in halfway through our day."

"I understand it's inconvenient, but this is the situation we're in right now."

"Leave my office now."

I get up and go into the break room for a cup of coffee. Two of the research assistants are there, and we talk briefly about what they did for the weekend.

Before I even have a chance to take a sip of my drink or put something in my stomach, I hear Dr. Johnson bellow for me. "Ms. Vargas, can you please come into my office again? Now." I roll my eyes and hope that none of the staff saw me do that. I debate if I want to just shoot him or push him off a bridge.

I walk into Dr. Johnson's office, and find he has two large men standing behind him. "What can I do for you, Dr. Johnson?"

He hands me a piece of paper. "Your employment here at Black Rock is terminated immediately. You're in breach of your contract."

"Excuse me? This is my company."

"According to this contract, because you're in breach of article 2C, your shares revert back to the company and, in essence, me."

I'm in complete shock, and I'm not sure what to do. Then my anger kicks in. "Dr. Johnson, I don't know what you're trying to pull here, but I own 51 percent of this company, and there's nothing you can do about that. How do you figure I violated confidentiality?"

"By posting false information on the internet. I guess you thought that, by sharing our research with the world, you'd be able to take credit for my patented delivery system and you'd be able to rid me of your company. Well, it backfired, and you are no longer part of Black Rock."

"I did no such thing."

He hands me a bunch of papers. "Here is my proof." Then he motions to the two men standing behind him. "These two gentlemen standing behind me are with the sheriff's office, and you have fifteen minutes to vacate the premises, or you will be arrested for trespassing."

I glance through the papers he's handed me. They are completely foreign to me. This is my research and I can see they are my notations, but I'm not familiar with these websites. How could they have been uploaded to these sites. "These are scientific sites with my notes, but I didn't post these. How did they get out? Who posted these?"

"You did. We traced them to your computer. Your time is ticking. You will be arrested if you don't vacate the premises."

"You will not be able to take this company away from me."

"Just watch me." He looks at his chubby, hairy arm and says, "Tick tock. You're down to eleven minutes."

I storm out of his office and go collect my belongings, packing up my bag and picking up a few things, including the most recent research that was put on my desk. I know I've been framed by that weasel, but fighting him right now isn't going to do me any favors.

As I walk out of my office, most of the staff is standing in the hallway, watching my nightmare unfold. "I'm very sorry about this." I don't know what else to say. They each hug me as I make my way to the exit.

Dr. Johnson announces, "Get back to work. I'm not paying you to loiter around the office. And, Ms. Vargas, you have fifteen seconds to leave, or you will be arrested."

After exiting the building and calling up a rideshare, I call Christopher. He answers on the first ring. "Hey, babe, what's up?"

"You're not going to believe what just happened."

"Good news?"

"Unfortunately, the exact opposite. Dr. Johnson seems to have created a reason that I'm in breach of contract and has fired me from my own company and is taking over all of my shares."

"Wait a minute. What are you talking about? How's that possible?"

I fight back the tears. "Can… can I come over to your offices and see if you can help me look at this? Maybe we can ask Sara to look at it too?"

I hear Christopher expel air from his lungs. "Of course, come as quick as you can get here."

The rideshare speeds across the thirty blocks to his office. As I stand in the waiting area, I take in his offices. Black Rock is so dreary in comparison. This place is slick—clean lines, open space, lots of glass that brings in the natural sunlight, and I see people smiling.

Christopher comes into the waiting area and gives me a comforting hug. That alone helps me feel a bit better. "Let's get you a drink."

I follow him to a room that is stuffed full of snacks and some leftover pizza that apparently was today's lunch. He points to a fridge with a glass front, and I can see almost every kind of beverage imaginable, including beer and wine. I think about a glass of wine, but I ask for a carbonated water.

"I know you had coffee this morning and probably a snack bar for lunch. What can I offer you here?"

I spot a sleeve of almonds and an apple and take both. "Thank you."

He grabs a sports drink and a package of peanut butter crackers, and I follow him to a small conference room. Sara waves and joins us.

After a tight hug, she says, "Christopher has only told me the basics. Tell me what happened."

I walk her through how we collect our data, how I leave it for Dr. Johnson most nights on his desk, and upload them to the company's secured cloud, about my computer being stolen, and I cry when I tell her how important this company is to me.

"Let's look at the partnership agreement and his supposed proof," Sara says in attempt to soothe me.

I hand her the "proof" of my deception and begin booting up my computer to pull the partnership agreement. While she looks through the print outs from the website of my data, she asks, "Is this your data?"

"I think so. It looks like my notations."

"Who has access to the secured cloud?"

"As far as I know, just the two of us—Dr. Johnson and me."

"Are you familiar with these websites?"

"I've never heard of them. I'm not even sure they are considered proven scientific sites."

"So, we wouldn't find you've posted on these sites before?"

"Absolutely not."

I look at one notation and see my name is Bella in these notations. "The strange part is, professionally I'm known as Isabella Vargas. Like your sister-in-law, I don't go by the name Bella except for family and friends."

"Interesting." Sara is taking copious notes.

While she reads the agreement, I fight the tears, and Christopher rubs my back. "You're going to be okay."

Sara looks at me, and I can tell she doesn't have good news for me. "Who was your attorney that drew up the partnership agreement?"

"It was someone Dr. Johnson knew."

"That's what I was afraid of. This is not to your advantage at all, and it's your research and the application of his method."

"So, what does that mean?"

"It's not good right now. The contract is written that while you may 'own' 51 percent of the company, he owns all the rights to your research outside of the company."

"I'm confused," I say. "Outside of the company?"

"Often companies will explore multiple ways for the drugs to work. In this case, if the company dissolves, he owns your research and can use it in another company."

I feel beyond defeated. I drop my head back and stare at the ceiling. *This can't be happening to me.*

I try to explain myself. "We were going into this like probably newlyweds do—going in with no expectations the relationship would fail."

"I'm not familiar with the websites he claims I leaked my research to. It doesn't make any sense that I would leak my own research. This isn't open source material. This is how to develop a cure, and it takes years and years of proprietary research. This is my PhD dissertation. It makes no sense." I'm almost yelling and people in the office are looking at me.

Sara lets out a big sigh. "I think you need to get your own counsel, and I think it's time that you pursue this with Dr. Johnson, if this is how you describe it. I have some recommendations you can consider."

I have no money. I doubt they'd take this work on contingency.

"Do you think it's possible that Dr. Johnson was the person who broke into your vehicle on Friday?" Sara asks Christopher.

"I don't know, but I think they were after Bella's computer since they left her bag with the research, my iPod, and thirty-dollars' worth of change in my car. They didn't even go after anything else of value," Christopher reasons.

Sara squeezes my arm. "I want to stress to you, this doesn't mean we don't have other avenues to chase."

I nod, but I'm not sure what those other avenues might be.

Christopher turns to look me in the eyes. "Did he tell you that he signed the NDA this morning and sent over financials to Dillon? He's also sent Cameron and his team some of the data you provided."

I shake my head, and I feel my world beginning to spin upside down. "I guess what you're telling me is that I'm totally out of the loop. How long have you been negotiating with him?"

"Nothing to worry about. We're going to get this fixed," he attempts to console me.

"You're negotiating with him without me. You knew I was the major shareholder. How is it possible that you would be going around me? We spent the weekend together, and it mysteriously didn't come up?" I'm beginning to go over the edge. I need to get out of here. I can't believe my world is tumbling down around me, and I'm learning that my boyfriend, who I've told about all of the problems in my company, has been negotiating with the person who is behind me losing my company. How is this possible?

I can't take this anymore. I need to get out of here. I thought he understood. I pick up my bag and purse. "I should go."

"Wait, Bella. We need to talk about this," he pleads.

"You can reach out and call or text me later. We'll see where we're at." I have no intention of ever answering his calls or doing anything with him again. I can't do this. I can't take this kind of disappointment, and he knew all along the situation with Dr. Johnson, and yet he continued down the path with him. I feel betrayed.

• • •

chapter

EIGHTEEN

CHRISTOPHER

This couldn't go more sideways if I had planned it. I pick up the phone and call Jim. "I'm going to send you over some material on one of the companies that were looking at. Their data was recently posted up on the internet, and I was hoping that you and your team might be able to track down where it came from. This would be more on a personal level for me, so you can send me the bill for it. This is regarding my girlfriend who we talked about on Sunday night. It seems they're doing exactly what Emerson suggested, and they're trying to get rid of her."

"Not a problem. We're happy to look at it."

"I just sent it to you."

"We've seen this happen before. I want to warn you that there are chances it can't be undone."

"I understand. I also think that, if he's the one behind uploading the information, then chances are he would be the one in breach of contract. It would also point out that we have a different issue going on and a company that wouldn't be a wise investment."

"It just arrived." I wait patiently while he looks at what was sent over. "Interesting. I'll have someone from my team check this out."

"Thanks, Jim. Her laptop was stolen from the back of my car on Friday night. It seems very suspicious. If we can find out where this is all coming from, that would be a great help."

"You reported the theft to the police?"

"Yes." I pull my cell phone from my pocket and pull up the information. "It's case 19-2947."

"I'll let you know what I find out. It may take a few days."

I need to make sure she knows that I'm behind her and support her.

Me: We'll get through this together.

I'm disappointed that I don't see the bouncing bubbles telling me she's responding. I debate my next steps, and I guess I need to share with Mason what's going on.

I knock on the glass outside his office. When he motions me in, I sit down and go through everything that's happened.

"Do you think we should continue to move forward with Dr. Johnson, or do we change and only invest in Bella, or just walk away?"

I know this is a test. He already knows what he wants to do, but he wants to see what I think. "Dr. Johnson doesn't know the material. They've lost their lab manager and their chief researcher, which in the end could mean, if we finance him, we'll be financing something that's going to go belly up."

He smiles at me, and I know I've given the right answer. "These things have a way of working their way out. Let's see what everybody determines when they look solely at their piece of the puzzle. Then we can decide what to do, but I agree with what you've laid out. So, if Emerson and Dillon have concerns, we need to rethink giving them any money."

I text Bella again.

Me: Hey, please call me back. Please?

I still don't see the bouncing bubbles, so I try a different tactic.

Me: Here's an update. I've forwarded all the information that you left regarding their reasoning for letting you go and what was posted on the internet to Jim. I'm convinced that Dr. Johnson was behind putting it up on the internet, and if we can prove that, that could get your company back.

Crickets. She doesn't respond, and I don't see bubbles rotating. Nothing. My stomach sinks. I desperately want to talk to her.

After work I go by her house. It's dark, so I know she's not there, but I knock anyway.

I text her again.

Me: I'm at your place. Are you home? Please talk to me.

Nothing. I don't know what to do. I'm completely at a loss. I'm torn between what we should be doing and what's not happening.

I don't sleep well, and I'm beyond upset and disappointed. I feel like I have lost my best friend in the whole world. We haven't been together long, but the loss is a crater.

I get up early like I would even if she was here, and I go for a run. It isn't the same without her, but I push hard. I wish she would talk to me.

• • •

A day turns into a week, and I still haven't heard from Bella. Jim gets back to me and says, "They routed through a server in Singapore, but it traces back to her computer here in San Francisco. But we also know it came after you reported it stolen to the police report."

"Is that enough to get her job back?"

"Unfortunately, it still isn't enough to say that she didn't set up to have her computer stolen, so we still need more time before we can determine whether or not Dr. Johnson was behind the break-in and the breach."

I can't help but be disappointed. I want the silver bullet to get her company back.

I spend the weekend in my underwear watching TV. Each time my phone rings or I receive a text, I jump to see if it's her, but it never is, so I don't answer or respond.

She connected with a part of me that others have never seen. I touched her and saw the reaction; it was beautiful and raw. For those moments, she was more real than the blood in my own veins, and I felt her like the beating of my own heart.

Without her smile, her laugh, or her joy, my world has become black, loneliness absorbing my every thought. My heart is broken where it was once soft, strong, and vibrant.

It's been two weeks since I've talked to Bella, and I've given up trying to reach out to her. I'm convinced she's blocked me and is ghosting me. I don't sleep well at night, and I have trouble getting out of bed in the mornings.

I see an invite in my email from Dillon. The subject reads, Black Rock. I've talked to Dr. Johnson multiple times, and he assures me things are moving along quickly. He doesn't mention Bella's departure, and I don't ask.

Picking up my file on Black Rock, I head into Mason's office and take my seat. Dillon and one of his new financial analysts join us, and we walk through the numbers in the financials.

As I look through them, I noticed they're different than the paperwork that Bella handed me. I search through my file and retrieve the list of overdue bills that Bella gave to me the day she was so upset. I hand it to Dillon. "You don't think he possibly could be cooking the books in order to show these to you?" I ask.

Dillon studies the paper I gave him and compares it to his notes. "This might explain a few things. We thought something was missing and the expenses weren't lining up. I see a few bills that were outstanding that are not accounted for in these books."

"Do you think he could be keeping two separate sets of books?" Mason asks.

"Well, anything is possible, but it does raise additional suspicions," Dillon replies.

Our meeting ends with Dillon planning on having Dr. Johnson in to discuss the financials, and he's going to ask about the information that we have.

I want to show this to Bella. I want her knowledge to counter what we're seeing.

I'm deep in thought when Emerson knocks on my door in the afternoon. "Hey, do you have a minute?"

"Come on in."

"We've interviewed the staff at Black Rock. They've seen quite an exodus recently. You mentioned that the lab manager was gone, but we also see a few others that have recently quit, and I was wondering if Dr. Johnson had mentioned anything about why this exodus was happening?"

I shake my head vigorously. "No. He hadn't mentioned that to me. In fact, quite the opposite—he tells me everything is fabulous and everybody loves it there."

"Okay, those are interesting rose-colored glasses he's wearing—so much so, they may be purple. From our interviews, I don't know that anybody loves it there. Most are new—meaning within the last two weeks. They are sending signals that they are looking for other work. My biggest concern is that they've lost the people with any depth of understanding and knowledge of the research and data, not to mention I'm definitely concerned about his leadership style."

"What can I do to help?"

"I'm just trying to keep you in the loop. I think at this point I need to push back a little bit on his team and goals for the company. I'm still not convinced his payroll even adds up correctly."

"Have you talked to Dillon?"

"We just briefly spoke about the financials. He mentioned a few of the bills were missing."

I chuckle. "Oh, you mean like the equipment rental?"

"Exactly."

"Do you feel comfortable sharing with me your feeling of what has you concerned about payroll?"

"It isn't a secret, but I'm not 100 percent sure that he's paid all of their payroll taxes."

"That's a red flag. Have you checked the state registers office to be sure?"

"I'm impressed you know about that."

"My dad owned a business, and I remember that coming up at some point."

"He was a patent lawyer, right?"

"At one point, yes," I tell her, not wanting to share all the sordid details.

"There are just enough things that it's not adding up for us."

I'm disappointed they got past me, and I feel like an idiot. They probably all believe I think with my dick, but it wasn't that obvious. There are so many things about Black Rock I wish I could remove from my memory. "I understand."

Emerson stands and looks at me with her brow knitted. "Look, I know you really feel like you need to put something down on the books. All I can tell you from my perspective is I'm not worried about what's going on. This is a new area for us, and we don't have a lot of credibility, which can make it difficult with some of these pharma start-ups. I know that you make money when we get new companies coming in the door, but right now I can't recommend Black Rock, and I don't want you to think that it's for any reason other than what I just told you."

"I appreciate that. I recognize I make money when the company makes money. If we give money to Black Rock and they don't do anything, then I don't make money. In fact, we all lose money at that point. So, I'm okay if we don't fund them. I'm so angry with Dr. Johnson from a personal perspective at this point that I'm not interested in funding them anyway."

Another week goes by, and I still haven't heard anything from Bella. I reach out to my best friend, Dave Morgan, and ask if he happens to have Ellie's phone number.

"Aren't you taking this stalker thing a little too far?" he asks.

"Maybe, but I have to at least try."

He sends me Ellie's number, and I debate calling but decide to go with it.

"Hello?"

"Hi, Ellie? This is Christopher Reinhardt. I'm Bella's friend."

"I know who you are," she says cautiously.

I can't take the chance that she hangs up on me and blocks me too, so I rush to tell her what I'm hoping she'll pass along. "She's not taking my calls right now, so I just need you to get her a message."

"Christopher, I'm not sure that I want to get in the middle of this."

"I'm not asking you to get in the middle. I just want you to share with her that we've gone through Black Rock's financials. They're not adding up. We have problems with some of the changes going on at the office. I think many people left in protest after she was let go. And the last thing I hope you'll tell her is that we think we see a problem with payroll tax payments. But the saving grace is that because she's no longer a partner, she wouldn't be liable for Dr. Johnson's malfeasance. I know that's not a consolation, but I just need her to understand it doesn't look like we're going to fund them, and we wouldn't do it without her being attached." I know I'm begging right now, but I have no pride when it comes to Bella.

She sighs loudly into the phone. "I'll pass along your message. But I'm not sure that it's going to matter. She feels you violated her trust."

"I understand. I tried very hard to separate my girlfriend from my business." I take a deep breath. "If you feel comfortable, please tell her how much I miss her."

"I'll let her know." I wait for her to hang up, but then she shares, "Christopher, we Latinas are proud. Don't give up on her. She was spread too thin and may not know how to back up gracefully when making a mistake."

My heart soars. "Thank you, Ellie. I'm not giving up. She means the world to me."

There's a lot of commotion going on for a Friday morning. I see people racing in and out of closed offices. Then I see Jim, the security consultant, arrive. I'm keeping my head down. I'm not interested in getting into anyone's crosshairs.

A meeting request for all partners in the large conference room is scheduled for ten o'clock. So much for staying under the radar. I busy myself with a new prospect called Everest Therapeutics. I see some similarities to Black Rock, since they are working on a Parkinson's drug.

When my notification of fifteen minutes until the meeting sounds, I wrap things up and drop by the kitchen to pick up a breakfast burrito and a cup of coffee before heading into the conference room.

All of the partners, plus our advisors, are present. This must be big. While we wait for Mason and, presumably, Jim, we talk about weekend plans. Dillon urges me to join him, Mason, and Trey for golf on Saturday morning. "Sure, why not?" I'd be in my underwear all weekend watching sports otherwise.

Finally, Mason arrives with Jim and two people I'm not familiar with. They are introduced as Walker Clifton, of the US attorney's office, and Cora Perry with FBI cybercrimes. I try not to let my eyes bulge as I share a concerned look with Cynthia.

"Thank you all for coming today. I've asked Walker and Cora to join us because we've received a threat from our hackers. They sent me a voice mail early this morning."

We all stop fiddling with whatever we are messing with and sit up straighter in our seats, anxious and nervous about what we're about to hear.

"Good morning, Mason," a computer-generated voice drones on in a monotone. "I see you and your friends at the US attorney's office have indicted us. We want to assure you, we are not scared of you and your indictments. You will have to figure out who we are, and none of you are smart enough to actually do that. We are everywhere, and you don't even recognize us. But we can assure you, we are not hiding. We are going to make a big impact, and you will regret the day our paths ever crossed."

The call ends, and we are quiet for a half second before everyone begins talking at once.

• • •

"What does it mean?"

"How do they know we got indictments?"

"Who could they be targeting?"

"Are they someone we know?"

Mason holds up his hand, and the room quiets down. "Walker, your thoughts?"

Walker puts his hands in his pockets and says, "I'd like Cora's team to review the voice mail." He takes a deep breath. "There are a few concerning things in the message. Obviously, the implied threat of a 'big impact' tells me they're mad and ready to take action. What that action is remains to be seen. Cora? What do you think?"

Cora clears her throat and is silent a few moments. "I am concerned about two things. The 'big impact' but also that they're 'not hiding.' If possible, I'd like to sit down with Jim and Cameron. I want to check each computer for spyware. I know you keep up with a vigorous firewall and anti-virus, but it may be time to apply some FBI anti-virus, and I hate to admit, I'd like to see some possible spyware of our own placed on each computer and employee cell phone."

Sara is the first to talk. "Cora, I appreciate what you are saying, but there are a number of privacy concerns when it comes to employees' personal phones."

"But also for company morale. This level of intrusiveness could really upset the balance we've worked so hard to cultivate over the last decade," Emerson adds.

"I agree with Cora's approach, and my thought is that my team can complete the installs remotely during the middle of the night, so we capture all the laptops that people take home," Jim interrupts.

"Good. And honestly, we usually hit cell phones by sending a link to each phone via an app we can create, and when the phone isn't in use, it will scan it," Cora says.

"I like that, but if you could give us some time to discuss this, that would be great," Charles suggests.

"I understand," Cora says.

• • •

We talk for a short while longer and head back to our offices. I'm not sure any of us will be able to work after all this.

chapter

NINETEEN

CHRISTOPHER

It's time to pull out the big guns. It could backfire, but it may be my solution. I need to reach out to Bella's mother. Google is my friend, and I find she's located down at the hospital in San Jose. When I call, they put me right to her voice mail and I leave a message. "Dr. Vargas, this is Christopher Reinhardt. My apologies for bothering you at work, but I was hoping I might have the opportunity to meet with you. I can come to you in San Jose or meet you anywhere in the Bay Area, and quite frankly, if you wanted to meet somewhere else, I'd fly wherever it was to meet you. I just want to check in and see how Bella's doing."

I remember Bella mentioning her mom left San Francisco to live close to her father and her sister. I also believe she's done some blood work on patients at a facility in Palo Alto. I take my chances and call. "Is Dr. Vargas a patient there at your facility, possibly a Parkinson's patient?"

The operator responds, "May I ask who's calling?"

"I'm a friend of the family. My name is Christopher Reinhardt, and I'm a good friend of Bella Vargas. Actually, she's my girlfriend, and I want to meet with Dr. Vargas to see if he would give me permission to marry his daughter." It's a little white lie. I'm hoping to pull on her heartstrings.

"That's so sweet. Yes, he's here. He's not able to have a phone conversation though."

"That's fine. I'd like to ask him in person anyway. What are your visitors' hours?"

"He can receive visitors between twelve and three."

"Great. I'll be down in a few days once I'm able to get it scheduled on my calendar. Make sure you don't tell him."

My afternoon is quiet, so I drive down. The facility is beautiful with an antiseptic feeling. It's definitely top-notch quality, and I can see they are really looking out for him. I sign in and I'm pointed to the memory care facility. As I walk in, I ask for Jose Vargas, and a nurse's aide points me to a man sitting at a table staring intently at a puzzle.

"Hi, my name is Christopher Reinhardt. I'm a friend of your daughter, Bella."

He's sitting in a wheelchair, and he has the shake that most associate with Parkinson's. "I… know… who… you… are..." I've come early in hopes that his memory is strong. He speaks incredibly slowly but leaves me with no doubt that he's in control of his memory.

"You do? That's wonderful. Your daughter's quite angry with me right now, and she hasn't returned any of my phone calls."

"Christopher…, you… need… to… understand… how… the… Vargas… women… work... They… can... be… real… hotheads…, but… they… get… over… it..." He smiles big, and it's infectious.

"I miss her. I just wanted to introduce myself and tell you how important she is to me."

"I… heard… you… want… to… marry… her..."

Ah, the woman who answered the phone ratted me out. "I do want to marry her—very much, but I know she's not ready. But I can assure you, I'm patient."

"She'll… come… around... She's… talked… to… me… about… you…, and… it's… been... a… long… time… since… she… talked… about… anything… other… than... her… work..."

"That's encouraging at least."

"She's… a… mean… cribbage… player... Come… back…, and… we… can… gang… up… on… her..."

I laugh. "I promise."

Meeting her dad tells me a lot about Bella. I need to get her back—whatever it takes.

When I return to work, I find Jim sitting in my office and waiting for me. "I'm sorry, did we have an appointment? I didn't realize I was missing anything. Please forgive me."

"No problem. Actually, I just got here and thought I'd hang out a bit to see if I could catch you. We just learned a few things, and I wanted to make sure that I shared them with you."

As I sit down, he opens up a file and I see photos of Dr. Johnson. "It seems that our friend Dr. Johnson's under investigation by the Lasker Award team."

I sit up straighter. "What does that mean exactly?"

"He's apparently being accused of fraud."

"Fraud? How?"

"From what we've uncovered, there is a scientist named Dr. Jeremy Sutherland who worked with Dr. Johnson as part of his graduate dissertation. He has presented evidence to the award team proving Johnson won the award for his research, which is corroborated by his advisor. Therefore, Sutherland owns the delivery system. He also presented the dissolution of the partnership agreement they had, where Johnson took the company away from him under false pretenses."

"Are you shitting me?" I sit back in my chair and think out loud. "This guy has a history of stealing scientific advancement from naïve grad students. What an ass!"

"Yes, exactly. He seems to attach himself to aspiring grad students and cheats them out of their work and possibly their doctorates. We think we have a lead on someone else he did this to, but we aren't sure yet."

"Man, what a jackass. Where is this Dr. Sutherland?" He points to a name of a company that looks familiar to me. I'm sure it's one that's come across my desk. I can't quite place it. "Do you think it would be okay for me to reach out to this guy?"

"Do you want us to pull his background?"

"No, I can start this off. I think, if he is smart enough to come up with the new medical delivery system, he's smart enough to probably have a pretty good start-up that we may want to fund."

"I like the way you think, Christopher." Jim beams.

Jim leaves, and I start looking through the proposals. Then I find it. Everest Therapeutics. They are in my maybe file. I see Jeremy Sutherland is the contact, and I have his number. I pick up the phone and dial him.

"Hello, this is Dr. Jeremy Sutherland speaking."

He's a bit formal, but that's okay. He's a nerd, but I'm one too. "Hi, Jeremy. My name is Christopher Reinhardt, and I'm with SHN. I received your proposal for funding."

"Oh? Err… yes? Um… what can I do for you?" he stutters, and it makes me smile.

"I was wondering if I could take you out for a cup of coffee and talk a little more about what you are looking to accomplish."

"I sent you a proposal." Typical nerd. He expects that what he's said in his proposal is enough. Most of the time proposals are written by sales people and technical writers. We run into this sometimes when a potential investment is nervous about their position.

"Yes, you did. I work in acquisitions concentrating in biotechnologies, and we are looking to add some pharmaceutical companies to our portfolio."

He's quiet a few moments. "I'd love to share with you what we're doing. I'm not sure we'll be a match for what you described, but we can talk about it," he says carefully.

I really appreciate his honesty. He's not a drug developer, which is why I moved him to the maybe pile.

We set a time to meet in the morning, and I send an instant message into Mason.

Me: Do you have some time today for a quick chat?

Mason: Give me until two o'clock?

Me: See you then.

I use my time to pull some information and prepare for my meeting. Mason isn't one of those who needs a lot of explanation, and he's great about letting us follow our instincts. Just before two, I pick up my research, grab the proposal from Everest, and stop by the kitchen for two cups of coffee and a package of the peanut butter crackers I watch him eat all the time.

He sees me and waves me in. "Thanks for your patience. We have things hopping with our hackers. Anyway, what can I do for you?" I hand him the coffee and crackers. "Thanks."

Sitting in the chair opposite of him, I share the Everest Technologies proposal and then hand him Jeremy Sutherland's bio. "I met with Jim today, and it seems our Dr. Sutherland has made a convincing enough claim about his medicine delivery system that the Lasker Award committee are withdrawing the Lasker Award from Dr. Johnson."

Mason's head snaps up at me in surprise. "Are you sure?"

"Yes, here's a scientific journal outlining the review."

"Wow, we really dodged a bullet with that one."

"Agreed. While Dr. Sutherland's proposal didn't merit an investment on its own, I was thinking we might want to partner Bella and Dr. Sutherland up. We could help the marriage along, and together they might have something phenomenal."

Mason takes a few minutes to review Dr. Sutherland's proposal. "I think that's a brilliant idea. I like the way you think. In the past when we set other companies up, it's been our best and easiest companies to work with, and they're always grateful that we put them together, so there's never any resistance when we suggest changes. And the best part is they are our biggest successes. Look at Tsung Software. Christopher, this could be a big winner for us. Do you think you can talk Bella and this Dr. Sutherland into it?"

"I'm not sure yet. Before I suggest it to Dr. Sutherland tomorrow, I wanted your thoughts."

"When do you meet with him?"

"In the morning for coffee, in his neighborhood on the north side."

"Would you like me there?"

"If it's okay with you, I'd like these first meetings with just me so I can develop a level of trust with them."

"Great idea. I'll put you on the agenda for Sunday night. This is brilliant. Well done, Christopher."

"I still need them to agree to this."

"If anyone can convince them, you can." He stands and walks me to the door and pats me on the back.

"Thanks, Mason."

I feel amazing, and this is a really big deal. I can't believe we may actually find a cure, or at least something to prolong Parkinson's patients' connectivity for the rest of their lives. Talk about making a difference. Why would I ever want to do anything else?

chapter

TWENTY

ISABELLA

I didn't realize how much of my identity was wrapped up in my job. I'm not someone's wife. I'm not someone's mother. I'm my job—a scientist, and without a job, I'm not a scientist. Granted, I'm working on my PhD and I'm still teaching classes. I'm not destitute, but the idea that I was doing something for a disease that has impacted my life so significantly really made me who I am, and without that, I feel lost with no anchor in the storm that is surrounding me.

After losing my job and walking out on Christopher, I can't stand to be in my apartment. I try, but it upsets me too much to be there. I float from Ellie's apartment to my mother's home, to my aunt's, and back and forth again. I'm focusing on being at the university and teaching. I'm trying to be present for my students—not worrying about being back at the lab or distracted by everything I need to do. My advisor meets with me and has a few suggestions on how I can salvage my research and still get my PhD, so I know it's not a total loss, but I still feel the loss of my company—which was essentially my child.

I've felt like I've been lost long enough. Before I head home, I go to the one place that I love the most. I walk through Golden Gate Park and enjoy the de Young museum.

In my family, we are either scientists or we are artists. My aunt has a painting hanging in the Impressionist room, but my favorite is the textile exhibit. The bright, vivid colors remind me of my neighborhood and my friends, but also the dresses from decades ago and the tapestries speak to me.

I stop and stare at a vintage Christian Dior wedding dress, and I take in the hand-beaded pearls and crystals. I really fucked up with Christopher. I know that I overreacted when I walked out, but I don't know how to apologize at this point without being too vulnerable, and I'm not sure I'm ready for that. Looking at the dress and admiring the sweetheart neckline and the crinoline skirt after almost eighty years, it's still jaw-droppingly beautiful but makes me sad. Walking with Christopher by my side and his defending me with my crazy aunts allowed me to think about myself getting married to him.

Wandering through the exhibits, I enjoy looking at the American art. I always see something new. Suddenly, someone roughly grabs my arm from behind and whips me around, almost knocking me off my feet. Coming face-to-face with Dr. Johnson, I'm shocked.

He stands too close to me, and I can smell the putrid breath and the raw onion smell of body odor. He has a glassy sweat sheen across his balding head and beads of sweat on his upper lip.

"What did you tell SHN about our financials?" he demands.

He speaks so quickly, I'm confused and not sure what he's talking about.

I pull my arm away from his tight grasp. "Don't touch me. I have no idea what you're talking about."

People are beginning to stare, and I'm grateful I'm in a public space.

"You told them things about our financials. You need to tell me what you told them, so our stories match."

Why would I do him any favors after he pulled the rug out from under me and stole my company and my dream? "Our stories don't have to match. You made sure I wouldn't be part of Black Rock anymore." I point at his sniveling chest as he breathes his awful breath at me in staccato bursts. "You need to go away."

He sneers at me, and I know I should fear for my safety, but all the anger I have replaces my fear.

"I am not going away. This is my dream," he says.

That's it. I take my finger and point it hard into his chest as I back him into the wall. "No! This was my dream. A dream you stole from me."

"If you screwed this up, and I don't get my money, I'm going to get even with you, bitch," he menacingly sneers at me.

The hair on the back of my neck stands on end, but I can't help but respond. "Go for it. I have nothing left. You've already taken everything from me that matters. I dare you." With that final remark, I turn around and practically run out of the museum and grab a ride back to my place.

I'm still shaking when I walk in my apartment. The air is stale from no activity in several weeks. I reach for my cell phone sitting on the table. I want to call someone and feel safe, but the battery is dead. Digging through my overnight bag, I find my charger and plug it in. While I wait, I go through the junk mail and pick things up. Once the charge gets to enough of a percentage it can function, it starts pinging like crazy. I have twenty messages in my voice mail and fifty-six texts. With a cursory look, most seem to be from Christopher and Ellie.

My unread email lights up, and I see an email from the old lab manager Jim.

To: Isabella Vargas
From: Jim Thompson
Re: My termination

Isabella, I got your voice mail and tried to return your call, but your voice mail is full. I wanted to let you know that I didn't quit. Dr. Johnson fired me. I'm sorry he led you to believe that I'd leave you hanging. He told me you both felt I wasn't moving fast enough. But now that I know he told you I quit, it's probably because I managed to stand up to him. I've heard through the grapevine that he recently took the company out from underneath you, and several of the team have gotten together and all quit in protest. Please know that if you are able to restart this venture, I'd love to join you again. I'll wait to hear from you, but I'm truly, truly grateful for the opportunity that you gave me at Black Rock. Finding a cure, or at least a drug that extends a Parkinson's patient's quality of life, means the world to me.

Jim

I looked through the other various phone calls and voice messages, and I finally take the time and sit down and listen to them. The messages from Ellie start out like usual—let's go out and move to more concern. I hooked up with her about a week after I disappeared, so she knew I didn't have my cell phone.

There are a few text messages from the team at Black Rock. They are text messages of solidarity and dismay over what had happened. I cry as I read them since they are kind and so supportive.

Christopher's messages begin with him begging to hear from me, and I feel terrible for not reaching out to him. I have such a level of sadness. My heart aches. I can't believe what this has done to him, and the fact that I selfishly didn't take my phone so I could recover will be difficult to explain.

My box became full so he couldn't leave any messages after about three days. But he kept the text message's coming.

Christopher: I understand you not wanting to talk to me, but please reconsider.

Christopher: Good night. I miss you so much. Dinner tonight at the Arnaults' was not the same without you.

Christopher: Dillon has gone through Black Rock's finances and something is off. Please call me.

Christopher: Have you talked to anyone over at Black Rock? Emerson says they have almost an entirely new team.

Christopher: I miss you.

Christopher: I'm not giving up on you. You're my everything.

Christopher: I met your dad today. He was funny. I liked him a lot.

Christopher: I know you don't want to talk to me anymore, but I may have found a solution for you to get you your end goal—funding for a new medication and your PhD. Please call me.

I can read how I've hurt Christopher, and that makes my heart ache. I'm still angry and disappointed about what happened but mostly because I lost my dream. I'm cautiously optimistic about what my future may hold, and for the first time, I debate reaching out to him, but my pride stops me. I'm embarrassed about what I said, and I still need to get myself together and have a good reason for my absence.

I rub my arm where Dr. Johnson grabbed me. It's going to bruise. Why did he think I told SHN about our books? Then I remember. I gave Christopher a long list of outstanding bills and our bank account balances. Mindy was always hinting that Dr. Johnson may not be what he promised, and I have a feeling she may have helped me sink Black Rock's position to get any funding. I smile. I can't help but like karma. I think it's going to be a good day.

chapter

TWENTY-ONE

CHRISTOPHER

The only thing I do other than work is go home and watch sports news or games on television, and twice a week I play basketball with the gang. Today I'm angry. I'm angry about so many things that have gone sideways and how much I miss Bella. Our game is usually well played but rarely aggressive enough that people get hurt.

Today we agree on a zone defense, and each time I get the ball, I play as if it's me against the other team.

"Christopher, you need to pass the ball."

I ignore Dave. I don't have to do anything, and if I can see a chance to score, I'm going to take it.

I step in front of one of my teammates to steal the ball and get knocked hard on my ass for being in the wrong place at the wrong time. I jump up and get in the guy's face. "What the fuck?"

"Dude, you're angry. Maybe today isn't a great day to play."

"Fuck that. I'm here, and I want to play," I yell.

"Next time," one of the other players says.

"Give me the ball. Let's go."

I feel a hand on my shoulder. "Not today, Christopher."

"This is fucked up." I storm off the court to the locker room. It's happened to most of us at some point, but I'm still mad they sent me out.

Dave follows me. "Hey, how about we go get a drink at Scotty's Bar?"

"Whatever."

I don't wait for him in the locker room to finish the game. I leave and head over to wait for him to join me at Scotty's Bar.

I'm half-way through my beer when Dave sits down. "How are you doing?"

I'm feeling defeated and lost without Bella. "It could be better." I think about it and seem to remember him mentioning he had a date tonight. "Don't you have plans with Ellie?"

He smiles. "I do, but she'll understand if I'm a little late."

We walk over to the bar and order him a beer and me a second. I buy, given it's my fault he didn't get the workout he was hoping for. The beers are cool and refreshing. Dave's a good guy, and I'm grateful he is hanging out with me.

I feel a tap on my shoulder. I turn and see Annabelle. "Hey," she says.

"Hey yourself. What's up?"

"I'm meeting my friends again, but when I saw you sitting here, I had to come over and catch up."

"That's very nice of you. I'm just sitting here drowning my sorrow's over about a breakup with my girlfriend."

"I'm so sorry. What happened?" I've never seen Annabelle so interested in anybody's life other than her own, and I somehow want to take the bait to pour out my heart to her and hear what sage advice she may offer.

"Dave, go find Ellie. Give her my best."

"Are you sure, man?" He looks at me skeptically to make sure I'm going to be okay.

"Yeah. I'll be fine. I'll head home shortly."

Annabelle smiles. She's drinking a pilsner. "What's going on with Bella?"

I walk through everything that went wrong in our relationship and tell her how much it hurts that she hasn't returned any calls, pouring my heart out to her.

"I just believe she is my soul mate, the one that I'm supposed to be with for the rest of my life."

She looks at her empty glass. "I totally understand. I feel that way about Mason. He's my everything. But I've learned over the last three years that I can't make him do anything he doesn't want to do."

"You're very kind."

"Don't let that get out. Everyone thinks I'm a bitch." She smiles and winks at me.

"I've never heard anyone say that." A white lie won't hurt her. No one trusts her, but to tell her that would only hurt her.

"Give her some time. She lost everything that she thought made her who she is—her company, possibly her doctorate, and you. She'll realize that the company and the doctorate are things that will bounce back, and hopefully she'll realize she still loves you before I set you up with one of my friends who knocks you off your feet—when you're ready of course."

Annabelle is really pretty sweet. I can see what Mason sees in her. She's about ten years younger than the rest of us, and I can see why the girls are protective of Mason. He's a nice guy, and he's worth some serious cash.

"I know this may be hard to explain, but there's an ache that comes and goes, always returning in quiet moments. I miss her so much, I want to talk and laugh with her like we once did, and her absence weighs on me. Maybe eventually we can be together again—close, happy... I've had my heart broken before, and I know it will eventually mend. I'm just not ready to give up. I still love her, and I'd come running if she ever needed me, but for now, our paths are going in different directions, and every step is difficult."

"That's very beautiful. I wish there was something I could do or say to make all of this go away."

"Thank you. I really appreciate your talking to me. I should get home. When are your friends showing up?"

"They came in a bit ago and are playing pool. They're fine." She stands on her tiptoes and gives me a hug. "Stay strong, Christopher."

I call a rideshare and wait outside the front door of the bar. I'm staring at my phone, looking through the pictures of Bella that I'd taken as we walked through the farmers market. She's so beautiful. I get lost in those dark brown eyes, and I desperately want to run my fingers through her hair. Because I'm distracted, I smell him before I see him. I'm startled at Dr. Johnson's presence.

He's mumbling, but I'm uncertain what he is saying. I should have reacted sooner, but it's too late as I feel the cold piece of steel through my shirt, pushing into my rib cage. He's rambling and drunk. I can smell his putrid breath, and he's looking at me, but there is nothing behind his eyes that show they are registering anything. He smells terrible, as if he hasn't showered in some time, and what little hair he has on his bald head is disheveled. I finally realize what he's saying. "You were supposed to be the one."

I have no idea what he's referring to, so I explain, "Vance, I'm not sure what you're saying, but my ride is pulling up and I need to go."

"You can't leave," he yells.

I push him back, making him stumble, and the gun in his hand discharges. My ears are ringing, and I see only the taillights of the rideshare as it speeds away. I don't feel like I was shot, but I'm not sure where the bullet went.

"Call 9-1-1," I hear someone say.

The gun crashes to the ground, and he scurries away. I stand there frozen as the police cars pull up with their lights and sirens blaring.

I hear, "The homeless guy who tried to hold him up ran that way."

Two officers follow where they were pointed, and another starts asking me questions.

"He's about five foot five and is as wide as he is tall. He's bald, and tonight he smelled terrible, like he hasn't showered in a while. His name is Dr. Vance Johnson. He is the founder of Black Rock Therapeutics." I explain the last few weeks of events to them and answer all their questions.

They're able to pull up the photo from his driver's license and ask me and the couple who were witnesses if this is the same man. Since I know him, I agree quickly, but the couple is slower to agree given his state when they saw him.

"Mr. Reinhardt, please be cautious of your surroundings. We are going to attempt to locate him, and when we do, we'll let you know, but meanwhile please be aware. You can go home now. We'll reach out if we have any other questions."

I nod and call up another rideshare. It's been a long day, and I'm glad it's over.

• • •

chapter

TWENTY-TWO

ISABELLA

I've slept ten plus hours each night for the last three weeks, and it's been amazing. I feel refreshed, and I'm thinking clearer. My brain is functioning, and I think I'm far less emotional. I make a point of getting out and running every day, attending a yoga class a few times a week, and I'm really managing my stress levels well.

I realize with this change in schedule that I need to make some changes in my life. As I sort through my junk mail and bills, there's a knock at my door. Since I live in a locked building, and I didn't buzz anyone in, I open the door, expecting it to be one of my neighbors. I'm surprised to find two gentlemen standing there.

"Ms. Vargas?" I nod, and they flash their badges. "I'm Detective Eric Lenning, and this is Detective Tim Gallagher. We're detectives with the SFPD. May we come in?" They look at me expectantly.

I'm nervous about what they could want. "Yes, I suppose so." I step back and allow them entry. "What's this regarding?"

"Dr. Christopher Reinhardt and Dr. Vance Johnson."

My stomach drops to the floor. What the heck could be happening? "Yes, please come in."

They sit down on my couch and interview me.

"What is your relationship with Dr. Vance Johnson?"

I explain our relationship.

"What is your relationship with Dr. Christopher Reinhardt?"

I explain how I met him and make sure they understand how SHN came to work with Black Rock.

"How did Dr. Johnson end your business relationship?"

I share how I believe he's behind the stealing of my computer and the person who uploaded the information to the internet so he could take my company from me.

"How do you think he fabricated the situation?"

I get up and fish my wallet from the bottom of my purse. I pull out the business card of the officer who we spoke to after Christopher's car had been broken into.

"Have you seen or spoken with Christopher since you were terminated?"

"No, I haven't. Unfortunately, I needed to kind of figure things out and get some sleep. For the last eighteen months, I've running on about four hours of sleep each night."

"When was the last time you saw Dr. Johnson?"

I hesitate to tell them what happened at the museum, but finally I do and show them my bruise on my upper right arm.

"Why didn't you report the assault to the police?"

I am shocked because I don't feel like I was assaulted. When I think of assault, I think of battery. I think rape. All he did was grab me by the arm and yell obscenities at me. Sure, I thought he was crazy, but I just brushed it off and came home.

"Were you aware he had a gun?" Detective Lenning asks.

I blanch. I had been direct and said things to him that upset him. He knows where I live. "No, I didn't know he had a gun. He just grabbed me and kept asking what I said to SHN regarding the bookkeeping."

"Would it surprise you to learn that Dr. Johnson is, how do I put this gently… obsessed with you?" Detective Gallagher says.

"Obsessed? How? Why?"

"From notes he's written, he seems to have been following you for some time. He has notes about seeing you and Christopher meeting behind his back."

"He was the one meeting behind my back. Why would he be following me?"

"He seemed to feel that you were the key to getting the funding for Black Rock and therefore his success. Does that surprise you?"

"Y-y-yes," I stammer. "I don't know why he questioned me about the funding and the challenges he was having securing the money from SHN. He took everything from me when he took my company. I learned recently through some voice mails and texts that they chose not to fund Black Rock, but my understanding is it's because he presented false records and bookkeeping."

"Ms. Vargas, were you aware that Dr. Johnson approached Dr. Reinhardt and brandished a gun?"

My stomach tightens, and I immediately ask, "Is Christopher okay?"

"Yes, he's fine. The firearm did discharge, and Dr. Johnson ran away. We're in the process of trying to locate Dr. Johnson. Do you know where he might be?"

I shake my head vigorously. "I think he lived close to Noe Valley, but I don't know that for certain." The tears begin to pool in my eyes. "Where is Christopher now?"

"He's not in the hospital, and as far as we know, he's probably in his own home," Detective Lenning shares thoughtfully.

I don't know what to do about Christopher. I feel conflicted about how I ended things.

"Ms. Vargas, be sure to be aware as you move around The City. He's upset with you and Dr. Reinhardt," Detective Gallagher emphasizes.

chapter

TWENTY-THREE

CHRISTOPHER

The sun creeps into my bedroom between the crack in the drapes and wakes me. It's early, but now that I'm awake enough, my mind spins out of control thinking about Dr. Johnson. I need to go for a run. It's going to be a full day, and I've come to have a love-hate relationship with running. My sister would tell you she loved to hate it, but I like the aftereffects of running. I just hate it when I'm doing it.

While I run, I think about my day ahead. I get it all planned out before I return home and get ready.

I've got a meeting with Jeremy Sutherland over at Everest Therapeutics first thing. We've agreed to meet in his neighborhood in North Beach at a coffee spot close to his place. When I arrive, I spot him right away; I can see how he'd be quite at home in a lab coat or with a plastic pocket protector in his shirt pocket with several pens. "Jeremy?"

"Yes. You must be Christopher?"

"I am. Great to meet you." I extend my hand, and he shakes it and makes eye contact. Score one for being not that big of a nerd. "Thank you for meeting me."

We get in the long line of people seeking out their morning caffeine hit. Grabbing our drinks, we sit down in the corner at a small table. He did apply for funding with SHN, so he's a little nervous.

I see the cover of the newspaper has a story about one of the Giants players, so to break the ice a little bit, I make small talk instead of jumping right in. "Are you a Giants fan?"

"I like baseball okay. If I had to choose, I'd go for the A's. And you?"

"I'm a Twin's fan."

"Are you from Minnesota?"

"I am—Minneapolis."

"I'm from Cedar Rapids originally, although, at this point, I've lived longer here in Northern California," he shares.

"I'm not there yet. I went to the U for undergrad and then to Carolina for medical school and my MBA."

"So you understand the science behind the pharma world."

"I don't know that I'd go that far. I understand what you're doing and the possible implications."

He smiles. "I appreciate your honesty."

"I'm hoping for some insight from you. Are you familiar with Black Rock Therapeutics?"

"Only on the periphery. I know they are using a method I was part of developing to create a drug for the treatment of Parkinson's."

"That's right. SHN was going to invest with them, and then something happened that I think you are familiar with." He sits silently, waiting for me to continue. "I understand you were truly the one who invented this delivery system and getting the drug to the brain, which Dr. Johnson took credit for and eventually won the Lasker Award."

He studies me carefully. "You're with SHN? Do you have any proof of that?"

I take my wallet out and hand him my card, and while he looks at it, I pull up the company website on my cell phone and show my photo."

"Sorry. After what happened, I'm reluctant to trust many people."

"I get that. We believe he did the same thing he did to you to the grad student he was working with at Black Rock. Can you tell me, how did you hook up with Dr. Johnson originally?"

"We were introduced by another grad student at Stanford. He was doing something unique with a drug that was used for a heart issue but was having a problem with the delivery system. My research showed it might be a good option for him. We worked together for some time. He was responsible for the drug, and I was responsible for the delivery system. His drug wasn't working because ultimately aspirin would be more beneficial than what he had developed."

I laugh because, in research circles, that is what people often say about failed drugs. "How did he take the delivery system from you?"

"I trusted the woman who introduced us, and she used my laptop to post some confidential information on the internet, and he used that to squeeze me out."

I sit up straight in my chair. "He did the same thing to the founder of Black Rock."

"I'm ashamed to admit, I know a lot more about Black Rock than I let on. I heard about what he did to Isabella Vargas."

"This makes my next question easier then. Would you be interested in having a conversation with Isabella Vargas? We at SHN like the drug she's working on and the delivery system you created. We may be willing to come up with the funding for you both if you consider a joint venture."

Now it's his turn to sit up straight. "What exactly does that mean?"

"If you two were to work together, SHN would be quite interested in helping you come up with a business plan and funding you that $300 million to get the drug to market."

"What does she say about this?"

"I don't know yet. We haven't suggested it. I wanted to see if you were open to the idea first."

I can see the excitement in his eyes. "I'm definitely interested."

"My thought is if we can put together a strong plan, SHN can help get you to market. We would be partners—one third owned by you, one third owned by Isabella Vargas, and one third owned by SHN. The two of you together have something that could really make it to market and be an absolutely viable company. It will be important that you both can work together."

"I'm absolutely interested in meeting with Ms. Vargas, and I don't care if she has her PhD yet. I've looked at some of the research that was posted online, and I know for certain she's smart enough, and she will get that PhD."

"Great. I appreciate your time today. You have my business card, and I will put the two of you in touch with one another."

"Wow, you've just made my day. Thank you very much. I'm incredibly excited. You know how to get a hold of me. I'll meet her anywhere she wants to meet."

• • •

Now I need to find Bella, but first I drive down to San Jose and meet with her mother. Why is it that just the idea of meeting with her scares me? Maybe because she was so direct with me when we met.

"Hello, Christopher."

"Dr. Vargas, hello. Thank you for meeting with me."

"I appreciate you coming to me."

She walks me back to her office, and I notice the walls are covered in her awards. She's a gifted doctor and very driven; I see where Bella gets it from.

"I understand you were behind getting Bella kicked from her company."

"No. That's not the case. I swear. Without her, the company has no value, so we're not funding it."

"I see. And what can I do for you?"

"I need to speak with Bella. She may not want to see me romantically, which kills me, but I met a man who Dr. Johnson did the same thing to, and I'd like to introduce them. He was the one behind the delivery system, and if they could work together, my company would like to fund them to get to market."

She looks at me thoughtfully. "She'd make a wonderful physician."

"I don't doubt that. She has your smarts and drive, but she also has an innate curiosity that would make the practice of medicine boring for her over the long term. She's a researcher, and the world could benefit from her skills and brains."

"I appreciate your candor, and you may be right. I'll also tell you, I'm not sure where she is. I think she went home to her apartment. She unplugged for several weeks and lived without her cell phone, so I'm not sure where she's gone."

• • •

Hearing that she's been without her cell phone makes my heart flutter. There is a possibility, even if only slight, that she hasn't seen my messages. "He was a jerk. He did it to another person. She may have been blinded by her passion, but she deserves this, and seeing a new drug introduced that could help Parkinson's patients would be a huge advancement in the treatment and care."

She stands, and I know I'm being dismissed. "Dr. Reinhardt, I love your enthusiasm. I know that you are good for Bella. Go find her, and help her get her cure out. Parkinson's robbed me of the love of my life. Others shouldn't have the same thing happen to them."

I'm looking over the Indian food that the company has provided in the kitchen for lunch today. It's late, and all that is left are the bare bones. I'm debating if I want the lamb masala or the chicken tikka, or maybe both. I can't decide as they both look good. Suddenly, a scream rings out, followed by some yelling. There are about five of us in the kitchen, and we all look at each other.

We have a lot of glass windows in the office, which gives privacy of sound but not of sight. When I peek out, I'm stunned to see Dr. Johnson, and he's waving a gun around. I whisper to the staff in the breakroom to get in the corner behind the fridge and stay put. The kitchen backs up to the elevators and has walls, so we're hidden from view. I watch Mason approach Dr. Johnson with his hand up, distracting him.

Across the office, Emerson gathers some of the employees and pushes them out through an emergency exit door as others leave the office through the back. Cynthia is also moving our employees out on the other side of the office. She makes eye contact with me and motions me to stay put.

I watch Dillon and Cameron approach the front desk. Dr. Johnson is almost incoherent. I pull out my cell phone and dial 9-1-1.

"What is your emergency?"

"My name is Christopher Reinhardt. I'm at SHN," I say and give her our address. "We have a man waving a gun around in our lobby. We've managed to distract him enough that we've gotten most of the employees out of the office, but there are three of the founders talking to him. Please send the police. Also, tell Detective Lenning that it's Dr. Vance Johnson. He was looking for him."

Dr. Johnson is getting more agitated, and I hear him screaming for me. "I need to see Christopher Reinhardt," he bellows. After handing the phone to one of the employees to stay on the line with the emergency operator, I walk out.

"Vance, are you looking for me? How can I help you?" I attempt to look him in the eye as I approach.

Cameron and Dillon block me from his view. I hate to tell them that a bullet will rip right through them.

Emerson grabs the receptionist by the hand and pulls her out while Cynthia empties the kitchen of the few people I left behind, leaving just the four of us to manage him.

Mason talks in a low, calming voice, keeping his hands in the air as he tries to talk Dr. Johnson into putting his gun down and having a discussion with all four of us. "But you can't do that with a gun in your hand," he explains.

"I demand to speak to Christopher Reinhardt. Alone," he yells even louder as he pulls the hammer back on the gun, his finger on the trigger.

I can't live with the idea that Mason, Cameron, and Dillon could be hurt because of me.

"Dr. Johnson, I'm right here. What is it that you need? Is everything okay?" I try to push forward, but Cameron and Dillon are a wall of shoulders, each over 6'3" and won't get out of my way so our view of each other is obstructed.

"No, it is not okay. The affair you're having with Bella has ruined everything."

Keep him talking. "What do you mean? I'm confused?"

"I've been following her. I made sure her car was towed when she parked it illegally at the university, and I hoped without a car she'd quit, but she just took the bus. I saw how you ate out with her and all the nights you spent together."

"Then you know she dumped me after you fired her."

"Yes, I do know that, but you ruined it for me."

"I can fix this. What do you need?"

"I need fifty million dollars."

"Dr. Johnson, your numbers don't equate to that amount," Dillon informs him. "You don't understand your business, and your books don't prove that money will help to bring your drug to market. It doesn't have anything to do with Christopher and Bella. This is not a good investment for us at this time."

We hear the police and fire departments arrive outside.

"It's all Christopher's fault. She was fine, working hard and blind to everything going on, until he came in the picture. This is Christopher's *and* Ms. Vargas's fault."

"That's not true," I tell him. "You presented the company to me as if you were always the sole person behind Black Rock. You indicated that Bella was merely a research assistant. Did you not realized we'd find out that she was the majority partner? Black Rock is registered with the state. You put me off from meeting her, so I came in on a random day. I didn't know that Bella worked with you."

He's definitely unstable, pacing back and forth and waving the gun around, but I continue. "Did you know I had met her once—a few weeks before I met her in your offices. I'd been searching for her. I had no idea she worked for Black Rock, and once I did, that's when our relationship started, Dr. Johnson. But she didn't have anything to do with the decision not to fund your company. We were going to make the decision regardless."

I hear the police coming up through the back stairs, and a voice yells, "Dr. Vance Johnson, please put the gun down and your hands up."

"I need my money," he bellows.

A police officer appears behind him and puts his finger in front of his mouth signaling for us to not reveal his presence. Dr. Johnson keeps wiping the sweat from his head as he begins to ramble.

"Her computer was never stolen." He begins to pace and is almost incoherent. He's mumbling more to himself than to us, and I can barely make out what he says. "I hid it under the passenger seat in the car. I put it there when she was at a party in Hillsborough. I would've done a better job of making it more obvious, except that there was a pack of dogs that came charging after me. I don't like dogs." He continues to repeat "I don't like dogs" and run his hands over his sweaty bald head. Now we know it wasn't a raccoon the dogs were chasing.

"Hey, Vance." I finally step around Mason and Dillon. He stops pacing and stares at me like he's confused, as if he can't figure out where I came from. "Were you the one that posted the research on the internet?"

In a moment of clarity, he spews, "Yes. Of course, it was me. I tried to get her to quit by making her life miserable, but she kept going. I fired everyone in the lab and hired incompetent people, and still she wouldn't quit. So, I decided to frame her. I needed her out of the company so I could have the money for myself."

"Why is it so important that you get all of the money?"

"Because that sniveling Dr. Sutherland has turned his research over to the Lasker Award committee."

"But what does the Lasker Award have to do with the money?"

"I need it to go down to Brazil without it I won't have enough money to hide in Rio."

"Why do you need to go down to hide in Rio?" I ask.

There is now a group of maybe six SWAT team members standing behind him dressed in black utility pants, helmets, and bulletproof vests.

"Because I'm losing the Lasker Award. I'm a laughingstock of the scientific community. This is the first time they've ever rescinded an award. Plus, they want the money back they gave me. Not only am I mortified, but I also don't deserve this, and I'm being bullied by them."

"You're not a laughingstock of the community, and you're not being bullied," I say, trying to placate him.

"Jeremy chose to leave the company. I didn't force him out. I was left to pull it over the finish line. That's what I do. I'm good at this. I manage things."

He seems to finally have a moment of clarity and sees that he's surrounded by policemen holding assault rifles.

As he turns around, the four of us are thrown to the ground by SWAT officers. Dr. Johnson lifts his hand with the gun, and we hear three sharp taps. Bam, bam, bam.

Dr. Johnson falls to the ground, a red pool of blood growing on his chest and a look of surprise on his face. It all happened so fast, I'm in shock.

chapter

TWENTY-FOUR

ISABELLA

I never watch television in the middle of the day, but for some reason today I need the background noise. I'm doing a deep clean of my stove when I hear there is something going on. Breaking into a talk show, a news reporter announces a hostage situation. When they share the cross streets, I know right away it's SHN. I'm positive it's Dr. Johnson, and I panic. I grab my purse and call a rideshare as I run down the stairs. I rush to the scene, and I'm in hysterics. Emerson spots me and runs over, giving me a tight hug. "Bella, are you okay?"

"Yes, where's Christopher?" I scan the crowd and ask again, "Where's Christopher? I'm so worried about him."

"Dr. Johnson is inside with Dillon, Mason, Cameron, and Christopher."

My eyes bug. The tears pool, and my heart beats rapidly. What if I never get to see him again? What if I'm never able to apologize to him for overreacting?

"SWAT is inside dealing with him," she assures me.

"Oh goodness, this is all my fault." My hand goes to my mouth as I cry ugly buckets of tears.

"No, Isabella, this is not your fault. You have nothing to do with this." She rubs my back, attempting to comfort me.

"I'm the one who brought Dr. Johnson into this. It's because of me he came to SHN for funding."

"That doesn't make it your fault. You can't control his mental health."

Her phone must vibrate in her hand because I don't hear it ring, but she answers, "Hi, Greer."

She listens a few seconds.

"Yes, it's the founder of Black Rock. We didn't fund them, and he's upset."

She listens again.

"I'd say this may make national news considering all the people who are here."

She listens once more.

"I agree. We do need to get out in front of this."

CeCe comes running up and hugs both of us. "Is everyone okay?"

"He has four hostages—Cameron, Dillon, Mason, and Christopher," I tell her.

Emerson ends her call and informs CeCe that Greer is going to try to get out ahead of this.

I've been so self-absorbed since I was fired from Black Rock, and I didn't know what I needed to do, but now all I want is to be able to see Christopher and hold him.

Three gunshots pierce the air, and a scream escapes me. Terrified, we look at each other helplessly.

• • •

We're all crying as Cynthia comes up to wait with us. We don't know what to do other than hold each other.

We hear over a nearby police radio, "Subject is down. The subject is down."

Looking up to the sky, I send a silent prayer that Christopher is okay. It seems like hours pass as I hold my breath and wait to see what happens next. I nearly fall to the ground in relief when I see Christopher exiting the building, followed by Dillon and Mason. I don't see Cameron at first, and that worries me, but then I see a redhead bolt from the crowd. It's Hadlee and she jumps into Cameron's arms. I run up to Christopher, and Emerson beelines it to Dillon. I'm surprised when CeCe rushes to Mason, and they hold on to one another.

"I'm so sorry," I cry into Christopher's neck. "I'm so, so sorry."

Detective Lenning walks up to us and says, "Would you both be willing to come down to our offices and have a conversation with us?"

I nod numbly, and Christopher agrees as well.

Christopher and I are escorted to the police station, and they immediately put us in separate rooms. They go through everything over and over again, asking the same questions in different ways. For three hours we're interviewed. They check our stories. I know my story must be much less interesting because all I did was see it on the news and come down.

I wait for Christopher to finish, and when he does, I rush into his arms and we hold each other tightly.

He takes me back to his place, and we sit next to each other with the sports news in the background.

"I'm so sorry for what I put you through," I say once again.

"No, I'm sorry for what happened. Nothing I did was meant to harm you. I always wanted you to have an opportunity for the funding to work with Black Rock."

"I understand that now. I was just stressed out, exhausted, and spread too thin. My feelings were hurt because I'd lost my company, and all I knew to do was run."

He takes my hands in his and looks me in the eyes. I see the warmth and love he has for me, and I know he'd never do anything to hurt me intentionally. "I have something for you to consider. Recently I met someone who I want to introduce you to." Christopher walks me through his meeting with Jeremy Sutherland and Everest Therapeutics, and I'm excited. I can't wait to talk to him. This looks and sounds like a perfect opportunity for us. Knowing that SHN is going to finance the adventure makes me happy, proud, and excited.

He kisses me, and a fire ignites inside me. Our kisses become feral and hot. I've missed him so much. He unbuttons my pants, and his fingers deftly move inside my panties, sliding along my crease. I break the kiss long enough to stand and pull my jeans off, and I watch as he undresses. I take in his hard chiseled chest, and his cock is rigid and ready, bobbing to wave at me. His fingers quickly return to my sacred channel and are magic inside me. My pussy is slick and wet, and his cock jolts instantly. I want everything. I want him inside me, and I want to taste his cum.

• • •

But he's much more patient than I am. He works my folds, presses my clit, and twirls two fingers deep inside me. I love the way he groans and huskily calls my name. I beg him to continue as he rubs his fingers deeper, finding the spot against my insides that makes my whole body arc like a cat in heat. Ground zero. My breathing comes faster, and I pump against his hand as his fingers go wild. Much as I'd like him to make me come, I know the pressure building at the base of his spine is too strong to ignore. He gives my nipple a final nibble before growling, "Now, Bella. Put that condom on." He points to a condom on the side table that I'm unsure where it came from. When I bend down to pick it up, I can't help but stop to lick the tip of his cock to taste him. I want to fuck him with my mouth, but right now, I want him inside my pussy, stretching me wide, even more.

I reach for the condom and roll it over his hard cock before straddling him and lowering my hot, wet pussy over him. It's been a few weeks, so it is a tight fit, but once I'm fully seated, we both let out satisfying groans as he completely fills me and then starts moving. The friction shreds my soul. He grasps my hips, pulling me down against every upward thrust. Faster and faster and faster and fuck!

It's painful. I have my head thrown back, my dark hair flying. My body quakes. Lips freeze in a half-open pout as I shout his name. He thrusts upward, hard, and lets out a bearish groan as my pussy clenches his cock inside me like a vice. My body shudders as my climax lets loose. His own hits so savagely he seems stunned. Gloriously my pussy locks tight, sucking every last cum jet out of his balls. It's so fucking good I'm lost to anything but him... but for us.

I collapse on top of him, gasping for air. He holds me tight, his dick still buried inside me, until we're able to breathe again.

I get up from the couch and go to the bathroom and then meet him in his bedroom. We lie together naked in our post-coital embrace.

• • •

"Bella, these three weeks without you were miserable. I know we haven't known each other long, but I want you in my life forever."

I look up at him, thinking how this feels right but also feels like it is going too fast.

"Will you marry me?"

I take a breath because I don't want to destroy him. "Christopher, I want you to know that I love you more than anything in this world, but I still think we need to date a little bit. We haven't even said the L word to each other." He's crestfallen. I lean in and kiss him deeply. "I'm not saying no. I'm just saying not right now."

"I can live with that. But know this, I am absolutely, entirely in love with you."

He kisses me deeply again, and when we break, I tell him, "I'm absolutely and entirely in love with you too."

"That's good enough for now," he announces.

I meet with Jeremy Sutherland, and I'm over the moon. We have complementary research styles. I ask him if he's considered a few options, and he has some things for me to consider as well. I'm confident we can pull this off, and we're close to an agreement and finalizing a partnership agreement with the help of Sara at SHN. She's looking out for the company, and therefore she's looking out for both of us—evenly. Sara encourages us to meet with our own attorney and have them explain what she's written. She doesn't want either of us feeling like we're being pushed or taken advantage of.

I sit down with my academic advisor and tell him where things are and what's going on in hopes that he is still comfortable sponsoring my dissertation.

"Isabella, I was always really nervous about what was going on with Dr. Johnson. You were working too hard for him. I'm really glad that everything is worked out. I'm thrilled with where you are going with Dr. Sutherland and would love to help you with your business plan and making sure that you get what you need to get your dissertation written so that you can defend this. You have an amazing mind, and I can't wait to be able to show the committee that you deserve your PhD.

I can't get over how excited and happy I am. As I walk outside, my cell phone pings.

Christopher: Hey, are you here on campus?

Me: Yes, are you here?

Christopher: Yes, I'm here. Come over to the north parking garage. I'm by the pay station.

Me: What are you doing over there?

Christopher: I have a surprise for you. Get your cute ass over here.

I'm shocked to see Ellie standing with Christopher, but what's even more surprising is they are standing in front of my hunk of junk. "Oh my God. How did you get my car?"

"Ellie told me where I could find your car. Sara helped us get it out of hock for free, and so we brought it up here for you."

I smile. "You know, I'm just getting used to public transportation."

"I'm really okay with you on public transportation because I'm concerned this car is a death trap."

I giggle. "I promise you, it *is* absolutely a death trap, and that's why it wasn't worth the twenty-three hundred dollars they wanted to get it out of the impound yard."

"Good, because right here"—he dangles an Audi key—"is the car that I want you to drive."

"I can't accept a new car from you. This is too much."

"I thought you'd say that, but I respectfully disagree. But in order to prevent a fight, think of it as my car you have free reign to drive. I want you to be in a safe car, and I think this is what fits you and your personality."

"I love you so much." I step in for a kiss. "Why didn't you just leave the car in the impound lot?"

"I know how stubborn you are, and if you really wanted it, I wasn't going to fight you over it. Not yet at least."

"That car's just dreadful. I realized that I get around just fine without it. We live in a big city where there is plenty of public transportation between MUNI and BART, and I can grab either a rideshare or a taxi when MUNI doesn't work."

"Before you two get all lovey-dovey, can one of you give me a ride home?" Ellie asks.

chapter

TWENTY-FIVE

CHRISTOPHER

Sitting on an airplane, leaving San Francisco headed to Minneapolis, I look at her. This is going to be a difficult trip. We've been together for a few months, and it's time I took her to meet my parents and my sister. My family is the polar opposite of hers. This could make or break us. "Are you ready for this? They haven't closed the plane doors, and we can get off and change our minds before it's too late."

She giggles. "It's going to be fine. No matter what happens, I still love you."

"Consider yourself warned. My family is crazy."

"You've met my family. Heck, my aunt even propositioned you. What could be more humiliating than that?"

"You'll see. But in all seriousness, my parents have no filter, and they think they're better than everyone else they meet."

She reaches for my hand and gives it a squeeze. "They can't be so bad because they raised you."

"That's debatable."

The door to the plane closes, and I sit back and pray that this weekend isn't the disaster I'm predicting.

The almost three-hour flight goes without issue. Bella reads periodicals, and I review several prospective companies' proposals.

As we are in final approach, Bella stares out the window. "It's so green."

"It's the 'Land of 10,000 Lakes,'" I say, sharing the state motto and license plate tagline. I point out the window. "That's the general area where my parents live."

"I can't wait to see where you came from."

After we land and work our way off the plane and through the airport, Bella announces, "You have the largest mall in the US and possibly the world, and you have a huge mall here in the terminal. Apparently, Minnesotans like to shop."

"Do you want to stop and do some shopping?"

"Not right now. I already know your parents are waiting for us. But maybe this weekend we can walk around the Mall of America."

"That sounds like a fun diversion."

As we enter the baggage claim area, I see Richard before he sees me. "Richard," I announce and give him a warm hug.

"Bella, this is Richard, our family driver."

Bella's eyes widen for half a second, but she recovers quickly. "So nice to meet you." I haven't quite explained my family to Bella. I didn't want to scare her off. Richard takes our luggage, and we follow him outside to his waiting car. As we drive across town, I point out several things that are special to those of us who are from here.

• • •

"Down that street is the Mary Tyler Moore statue that is from the show where she hails a cab. And this park has a magnificent waterfall that's all natural. I'm hoping we can stop by this weekend. Here is the U. I went to undergrad here. There are fun tunnels that connect all the buildings, so we can hang out there and get lost."

I love that she nods and is excited to sightsee. A small part of me loves this town. It's a great place to raise a family, but I can't stand the winters. It's just too cold for me. We really aren't here for very long, but if it goes well, we'll come back.

I see that Richard is taking the long route. "Not in a hurry to get to the house, Richard?"

"No, sir. I just thought the scenic drive would make a better impression on Miss Bella."

"You're very sweet, Richard. Thank you," Bella says.

Pulling past the gates and into the driveway, I see the house. It never changes. It stands quite stately. It is bigger than it looks from the outside—and it looks big from the outside. The walls are uneven rough rocks, the roof arched bricks.

Hazel, our housekeeper, opens the door to greet us. I lean in for a warm hug. "Hazel, it's great to see you."

"I'm so grateful you're here. We miss you so much. It's just not the same in the house without you," she says with great affection in her voice.

"Hazel, this is my girlfriend Bella." Turning to Bella, I say, "Bella, this is Hazel. She virtually raised us." She blushes, and I put my arms around her. "I missed you too."

I hear my mother walking down the hall. "Yes, Hazel raised you, but you act like I had nothing to do with your childhood."

"Hello, Mother. You look beautiful as always."

She smiles brightly. She's wearing a navy St. John Knits skirt and blazer with a low Ferragamo heel. It's her typical uniform. She holds both my arms and comes in for an air kiss by each cheek. There's very little warmth in her touch.

• • •

"Welcome home, sweetheart." She pulls back and looks at Bella with her eyebrows raised.

"Mother, I'd like you to meet Bella." Again turning to Bella, I say, "Bella, this is my mother." Bella starts to walk in to hug her, and my mother sticks her hand out to shake her hand. I look at Bella and just shrug and shake my head, embarrassed for my mother.

I can hear voices in the back of the house, and my father comes forward. "Father," I acknowledge.

"It's good to see you, Christopher. I'm glad you finally made it home. Who do we have to thank for that?"

"Father, I'd like you to meet Miss Isabella Vargas, but you can call her Bella."

He extends his hand. "Nice to meet you, Isabella."

I shake my head. My parents don't realize what pompous jerks they come across as all the time.

My father motions for us to follow him. Two steps lead down to the sunken living room decked out in plush, vibrant furnishings in golds and browns and pale blues. Brick columns separate the cozy living space from the dining room, and beyond is a modern kitchen with granite counters.

I spot my brother sitting with his feet up on the coffee table. My mother throws him a warning glare, but he doesn't move his feet until Hazel walks into the room. Then I see my sister and her long-term boyfriend. I'm convinced they are only together to please both sets of parents and that Alex is actually gay and my sister is his beard.

My brother stands. "Hello. I'm Stephen, but you can call me Stevie. Everyone else does."

"Your father and I call you Stephen," my mother says with in an exasperated tone.

He leans in and whispers, "Stevie."

"This beautiful woman is my sister, Margaret, and her boyfriend, Alexander."

"Nice to meet you," Bella says.

"Please call us Maggie and Alex," my sister says as she comes in for a warm hug.

My patience for my parents is quickly waning. I need a drink, and it's like Hazel can read my mind. "Master Christopher, may I get you a predinner drink? Maybe a beer?"

I turn to Bella and say, "What would you like for a predinner drink? Trust me, you'll want one. I was thinking scotch. What do you think?"

"A white wine is fine."

My mother smiles because that is all she ever drinks.

Hazel quickly returns with our drinks, and we all sit around the living room. My father drones on about the business and then stops when it occurs to him he doesn't want to let out any corporate secrets to an interloper. "Miss Isabella, what is it that keeps you busy?"

"I'm a doctoral candidate at the University of California in Berkeley."

"And what is your area of study?"

She smiles. "I'm studying for biochemistry."

My father gets a puzzled look on his face. "What do you expect to do with that?"

"Pharmaceutical research. I'm working on a new drug for the treatment of Parkinson's disease. My father has Parkinson's, and while I most likely won't come up with a drug for him, maybe I can prolong the life of someone else's father."

My father turns to me and says, "Good to see you found a smart woman. Maybe she can get you to use your medical degree or move home and take over the family business or maybe both."

"Father, don't start with me. I told you that I wasn't moving home. I was only bringing Bella home so you could meet her."

"We just want you here and close to the family," my mother says. "It is important for you to take over the company."

I see the confused look on Bella's face. "What's the family business?"

Maggie was taking a sip of her drink and almost spits it across the table at Bella's question. Stevie turns to Bella and says, "My brother hasn't shared with you our family business?"

Before I can answer, Bella says, "No. Are you undertakers?"

Maggie laughs. "I really like this girl."

My mother speaks up and proudly says, "No, we are in the retail business. We own three department stores."

"Department stores?" Isabella is confused, and then her eyes pop. She's put some of it together.

"Yes, my paternal great-grandfather started Reinhardt Dry Goods. My maternal great-grandfather started Hudson's. They arranged the marriage of my parents, which made Reinhardt Hudson's."

Her lips become a tight line. I know I should have told her before we came, but I couldn't figure out how.

"My grandfather disliked Sam Walton, the founder of Walmart, so much he decided to start his own five and dime store."

Isabella looks shocked.

"But there's still one more. My grandfather had a long-term mistress, and he named a midlevel department store after their love child, calling it Murphy's," Maggie shares salaciously.

My mother interjects, "That is not true. He started Murphy's for his long-time secretary as a sort of a pension for her and her son. Unfortunately, her son died in the Vietnam War, so it is all run by my husband. We have three department stores for all economic classes."

I'm embarrassed by how specific my mother is being. She turns to Bella and says, "Well, apparently my son did not want to tell you that he is independently wealthy."

"I'm not independently wealthy, Mother. I inherited a bunch of money that sits in a trust fund that I don't touch. I insist on earning my own way," I explain.

"I hope you told her you are expected to come back and take over the business," my father says.

"What's wrong with Stevie or Maggie taking over the family business?" I demand.

My father turns to me and says, "Because it is designed to be run by the firstborn son."

"You loved being a patent attorney until Grandfather died and left you the business. I saw what it did to you, and I'm not interested in taking over the business. I'd like to make my own way in life. I'm not interested in my trust fund. My expectation is that it'll be something that I can pass to my children one day, as it was passed to me, and that for generations from now no one will ever touch it. It's only emergency money."

"You have such lofty ideas. California is really wearing off on you," my mother says with bitterness.

"Like the liberalism in Minnesota? Mother, give me a break."

Hazel rings a bell and announces dinner is served. When I sit in my place, Hazel puts her hand on my shoulder, and with Bella beside me, I calm down.

My father talks about the business during dinner. It's boring, but Bella is polite and asks the occasional question. Alex just sits there. It's like he isn't even in the room.

I don't care who runs the business quite frankly. I know that I own shares of the stock store, but I couldn't care less.

Watching paint dry would have been more entertaining than dinner. When we finally break for the night, I lead Bella upstairs. I show her my childhood bedroom. It's been redecorated since I moved out at fifteen.

The wide French doors open to a patio and dark view, and to my right I watch as Bella pushes another door open. Flipping on the light, she said, "This is the bathroom? This is bigger than my entire apartment at home. We can even take a bath together in here."

My mother enters the room. "Bella, your room is down the hall."

"Oh, that works." She walks over to her bag and picks it up.

"Mother, Bella is going to stay with me here, or we'll go stay at Kenwood Manner."

"Christopher, it's your mother's house, and we're guests. I will stay wherever she asks," Bella says firmly.

My mother turns to lead her to her room, and Bella gives me the evil eye. When my mother returns, she says, "I like her, but I need to you to at least pretend you're moving back here to take over the business. Your father's health is very precarious right now, and he doesn't need the stress of your plans to not take over the business."

"I don't know why that's a surprise to him. He's known since I was fifteen that I have no desire to touch the business."

"That's a lot of water under the bridge." She's been in the middle of this fight for almost fifteen years, and I know it exhausts her. "Good night, Christopher."

"Good night, Mother."

She shuts the door behind her, and I give it a few seconds before I go in search of my girlfriend. "Hey," I say as I knock on her door. She's dressed in cotton plaid sleep pants and one of my Carolina T-shirts.

"We probably have a few things to discuss," she puts her e-reader down in her lap and looks at me critically.

"I know. I just didn't know how to approach it. Usually people ask if I have anything to do with the department store, and that is how I approach it."

"Fair enough. It's a difficult topic. Not always easy to say, 'I'm a billionaire heir to the Reinhardt retail fortune.'"

"You're funny." I tickle her lightly, and she squirms away. "You had a great relationship with your dad. I didn't. I moved out of here and in with Hazel and Richard when I was fifteen and applied for formal emancipation. They took care of me. I went to the U because there is an endowment there, and I went to medical school on loans until I was old enough to control my trust, and then I got out of debt. That's the only time I've touched that money. I also have no plans to do anything more than give it to our children one day. I was serious with my mother. That money is for emergencies."

"I'm good with that, but I think your family needs you, and you need to figure out how to be here for them."

"I'll make my father feel like I'll take over the business. Stevie, Maggie, and I all agree that once my dad steps down from Reinhardt Hudson, we will hire someone who better understands the business and can take us into the digital world."

"Good. Give me a big kiss, and then I will meet you in the morning."

I kiss her and our tongues do a delicate tango, making me moan. "Please let me stay with you tonight and do all sorts of naughty things to you." My hand moves under her T-shirt, and I massage her breasts.

She nips at my bottom lip. "I'm a guest in this house, and your mother was very clear we had our own rooms."

I leave, and I'm sure I'll have blue balls for the rest of the night.

I wake before Bella does. She deserves the sleep, so I let her be. I walk downstairs and find the family has been up for a while because they are more accustomed to the time difference. I see my brother sitting at the kitchen table. "Hey, what brings you home?"

"You. I'm just here to watch more family drama. This is more entertaining than anything I could watch on television."

"Aren't you funny. Don't worry about us, we'll be fine," I assure him.

"Did Mother tell you about Father?"

"Yes, she told me that Father is dying, but hasn't he been dying for years?"

"I think this is different. I think the cancer has spread, and he's refusing treatment this time," Stevie says quietly and with some concern.

The news is a mixed bag for me. Part of me is indifferent. He stopped being a caring father once he took over the business, and the other is scared for my mother and our family.

"I can't do this, Stevie. You need to understand. I don't like this business. But honestly, if you wanted to take it over, I'm really okay with that. You can even have all my shares. I—"

"Good grief, retail is awful. I don't want the business, and I'm positive Maggie doesn't either. When you suggested hiring a CEO from outside the company, and we would just advise, I think she celebrated, but this has been hard. It's not been going well because of Father's health, and he's carrying a lot of stress over the business struggling as our competitors continue to close stores and go out of business."

"None of us have a passion for the business, and all we'd manage to do is drive it into the ground. We'll work it all out. But this weekend isn't about that. I want Bella to meet everyone, and I'm getting Grandmother's ring and proposing."

He pats me on the shoulder. "She's smart, beautiful, and she held her own with Mom. She's perfect for you. Congratulations."

We spend the afternoon exploring the Twin Cities, and I take her by where I went to school and my favorite restaurants. Our waitress in is a short black skirt and a tight black shirt that hugs every curve and shows a lot of cleavage. "I can see why you really like this restaurant. The girls here don't leave a whole lot to the imagination," Bella quips.

"The food's outstanding," I assure her.

"Everyone here is blonde. Is there such a thing as a brunette in this town?"

I look around and laugh. "We are all descended from our Nordic ancestors. Our winters scare dark-haired people away, so we all tend to have blond hair."

"And beautiful blue eyes," she adds with a salacious smile.

"True, we have to import brunettes."

"Are you planning on importing me?"

I look at her thoughtfully. "I don't think so. I really don't feel like this is my home anymore."

"Do you know where you want to go?"

"I want to be with you and for you to find a cure for Parkinson's with Everest Therapeutics."

"Despite what you think about your family, this has been a good trip, don't you think?"

"Absolutely. I can't say that I'm in a hurry to come back during the winter. I don't miss the cold here. But we still have to go shopping at MOA."

"MOA?"

"Mall of America. We'll head out after lunch and go before we fly home. I hope you're not too disappointed."

We head to a park and walk down the path holding hands. People stop and stare at her. Bella is beautiful. I can't help but feel eight feet tall knowing that this woman holding my hand loves me. We stop by the waterfall. "This is not a man-made waterfall—it's very natural."

"It's beautiful," she says.

"Thank you for coming this weekend. I just want you to know that you mean the world to me. I didn't know what love was until you came into my life. I thought it was something you read about in a book. Something intangible. I certainly never learned it from my parents. But you changed all that. You changed everything with your mesmerizing smile and your sweet, unfailing compassion. You taught me how to love, and you saved me. You saved me from something I never wanted to be. Every single day you make me want to be better than I am. I'm nothing without you, Isabella." I pressed my forehead to hers. "Marry me. Please?"

I take out my grandmother's single carat, center-stone diamond ring surrounded by pavé diamonds.

She kisses me. "I'd love to marry you, Christopher Erikson Reinhardt."

chapter

TWENTY-SIX

ISABELLA

"Are you serious? His family wants him to move home and take over the family business?" Ellie asks.

"Yep. Because he's the firstborn son," I explain to her and tell her the plan Christopher and his siblings have devised to keep the business afloat, and she's shocked.

"No wonder that boy is always so well-dressed. No joke, it explains a lot." She looks around the coffee shop. "So, when are the girls supposed to get here?" Ellie looks at the time on her cell phone and bounces in her chair. "I'm so excited for you. I can't wait to see what wedding dress you choose."

Once we have our coffees, we walk the block and a half to the dress shop that CeCe's personal shopper recommended.

The girls are asked to take a seat surrounding a round stage with mirrors, and I am supposed to stand on the riser so I can see almost all angles of anything I try on.

The fitter takes both my arms, opens them wide, and turns me around. "I have some suggestions for you in the dressing room."

She follows me into the dressing room—so much for privacy. Hanging are four beautiful dresses.

She helps me into the first dress. It's an A-line that is sleeveless with a natural waist and beautiful lace. I admire the dress from all angles.

"The train is buttoned up, but once you step on the stage, I'll unbutton it for you to see."

She follows me out, and the girls all stop midsentence.

"You look beautiful."

"Stunning."

The fitter unbuttons the train and positions it. She then points out the satin ribbon at the waist. "That can be changed to a different color for your reception."

I turn in a complete circle, admiring the dress. "It's beautiful," I whisper.

She gathers the train and follows me to the dressing room where I put the second dress on. It's a traditional ballgown—strapless with a dropped beaded waist and backless.

I walk out to the stage. The fitter fluffs the skirt a bit, and I feel like a giant puff.

"I like the first one better of the two," Ellie announces.

Everyone seems to agree.

I return to the dressing room and try on the sheath dress. It's a little tight across my hips. The fitter whispers to me, "Don't let that discourage you. Any dress you pick would be customized to your body. You have a perfect hourglass figure with narrow waist, a nice bust, and great hips."

We walk out and again she undoes the train. It's quite lovely in a cream. The front scoop neckline really makes my breasts look rather big.

"I'm not crazy about the feathers," CeCe announces.

"But the dress design will leave every man in the room with a raging hard-on," Ellie declares, and the room breaks out in laughter.

"One more dress," I announce.

I walk back and try on the mermaid dress. I hate it immediately. Not only is it really tight at the knees, but once it opens up, the ruffles are huge. The fitter says, "Not my favorite dress, but it's very popular."

"Do you happen to have any short dresses?"

"I do. They're great for receptions."

"That sounds perfect."

I walk out in the mermaid dress and show it to the girls. It is a quick and unanimous "No way!"

The fitter pulls another dress for me to try on.

Once I see it, I don't even have to try it on. I know it is perfect. "How did you know?"

"Try it on first."

It is a white lace dress that stops above my knees. It's a sheath with a natural waistline, and the crystal beading is subtle and everything I've ever wanted.

I don't care if the girls like it, I'm getting it. Plus, compared to ten thousand dollars for the other dresses, this one is only two thousand. Still more than I want to spend on a dress, but I really feel like I can wear this dress again.

As I walk out to the stage, the girls all admire the dress.

"Wow! That dress was made for you," CeCe admires.

"You look beautiful," Emerson says with awe.

"It's totally you," Ellie fawns.

"Perfect for a reception." Greer nods her approval.

"I think we need to head to lunch," I announce.

Emerson replies, "Good because I have a reservation over at Laurel Court in the Fairmont for high tea in an hour."

"So very girly. I love it," I announce.

Lunch is perfect. We have a nice afternoon, and we spend a lot of time talking about CeCe's latest boy toy.

"You mean he's a real prince?" Ellie asks.

"Yes, but his brother is the king and has three kids, so he's fairly far down the food chain as far as succession goes. He lives here in San Francisco and went to a boarding school back east for high school and then to Princeton."

"Have you met his family?" Emerson asks.

"We flew back last month. I have to admit, he is fun, but he doesn't really work, so I'm not sure how long I'll keep his interest."

"Well, given you work hard, that could be a problem."

"He may not be the one. I'll find the right man eventually," CeCe declares.

"I have to ask, after Vance Johnson took the guys hostage, I saw you go running into Mason's arms. What was that about?" I ask.

Everyone looks at each other as if I pooped on their corn flakes and asked them to eat a big spoonful.

"Mason and I have a great friendship. We've been friends for ages. He lives with Annabelle, and I suspect they're going to get married here soon—maybe even before you."

"I'm sorry. It's none of my business, but you two just seem to fit so well together."

"I think we're better friends."

I can't help but think I see a bit of hurt in her eyes. I'm sure she likes Mason, but he's all caught up with Annabelle. What a fool.

chapter

TWENTY-SEVEN

CHRISTOPHER

SHN plans an annual party for our clients and staff. We played with the idea of doing it on a cruise ship this year, but Greer reminded us about a difficult client and asked, "Where are you going to go if he gets his hooks into you for a whole weekend?"

So when CeCe and I realized we have a friend in common and he's opening a casino in Las Vegas on the strip, the party was moved to accommodate the opening of the casino. He even went so far as to do the soft opening with our company and clients. We've booked over one thousand rooms, and Jonathan, the owner, is using the party as a chance for his teams to practice and work out some of their kinks before they open all three thousand rooms.

On the ride to the hotel, I kiss Bella on the forehead and asks, "Are you sure you don't want to plan a big church wedding?"

"No, I like the idea of a surprise elopement."

When we arrive, and Jonathan is waiting for us. "Christopher, so great to see you. Welcome to the Shangri-la Hotel."

"I'm incredibly impressed. It looks amazing," I enthusiastically tell him.

"I agree. Thank you for allowing us to reserve so many rooms," Bella adds.

"It wasn't even a third of our rooms, so it's perfect to launch." Jonathan leans in and whispers, "Plus, to host all of the top entrepreneurs of Silicon Valley is huge. It's you that I owe."

"I know everyone will have a great time, and I believe our PR person did a pitch to the San Jose and San Francisco newspapers, so you may even get a little bit of publicity out of this for a while."

"Thanks, man. We've run ads in all the travel mags and major travel sections. I'm feeling pretty good about us."

"Everything is still pretty much under wraps for the party tomorrow night?"

"Your party planner is amazing. I tried to steal her away and hire her to come work for me full-time, but she turned me down flat."

"Tina is top notch, but I think we have something you don't," Bella shares.

"What is that? Maybe I can find it here in Vegas. Everything is here," Jonathan plots.

"Well, that's hard. We have her sister working for SHN, and all of her family is in the Bay Area," I tell him.

He closes his eyes and looks to the ceiling. "You're right, I don't have anything even close to that."

Tina walks up and gives Bella a big hug. "I'm all ready for tomorrow night."

As Emerson walks over, I whisper, "Great."

"Tina, I love the gift bags you are giving to all our attendees," Emerson gushes.

"Thank you. Have you met Jonathan Best? He's the owner of Shangri-la."

She lights up. "No! Thank you so much for allowing us to have our annual party here. I heard that the airport had no more room for private plane parking, so they were dropping people off and heading to airports close by."

"I think that's a good problem to have. We should be ready. What's first on your agenda?" Jonathan asks.

"We have a reception tonight, and several acts from Cirque are coming to perform. We're expecting you," Emerson tells him pointedly. "I would like to have you introduce the band tomorrow night."

"Are you kidding, the biggest band in the world? I wouldn't miss it. I've made sure to put them in a great suite, but Christopher here gets the best. I have to thank him for putting us on your radar."

"He deserves it," Emerson says warmly.

"What are the plans for during the day tomorrow?" Jonathan asks.

"We have a golf tournament. The person who can beat Emerson will get a big prize—but they don't know that yet," Tina shares.

"Are you that good?" Jonathan asks, turning to Emerson, causing her to blush.

"She's that good," I assure him.

"Tomorrow night is the big party," Tina continues. "And the spa is pretty much booked out all weekend."

"Speaking of," Emerson says, "I need to steal Tina away, can you excuse us?"

We nod.

Turning to me, Jonathan asks, "Is Maggie coming?"

"Yep, and Stevie too. My folks were on the fence, so it's a fifty-fifty shot they'll be here."

"You didn't tell them why they needed to come?" Jonathan asks incredulously.

"I hinted pretty heavily, but you know them. Hazel and Richard will be here at least, and that's all that I care about."

The party with a famous DJ is a blast. I dance the night away. Ellie is still seeing Dave, and they only have only eyes for each other.

"I think Ellie and Dave may be next," Bella elbows me and nods at them.

"I might know that you are correct, but I think he's waiting until we marry to pop the question."

"Good, then we know that will be happening soon."

Looking over to CeCe and her prince, I see they are awfully snuggly together. "You know that guy's actually a real prince, right?"

"Really? Where are his bodyguards?"

"If you look closely you'll see them. They do a fantastic job of blending in."

Cameron and Hadlee are sitting with a group of tech entrepreneurs. Cameron's a rock star in this world, and they are hanging on his every word. Many of these guys were saved by his genius and would probably take a bullet for him.

Emerson is dancing with a group of girls I don't recognize, but I think it's her staff, while Dillon and Mason look on with Annabelle by his side. Annabelle catches my eye and gives me a thumbs-up. I smile so big. I don't think I've ever been this happy.

This weekend is going to be a blast and, not to mention, full of surprises for almost everyone.

I head out at seven for our tee time. It's hard to leave Bella sleeping soundly in our bed. With the busy day ahead, I won't see her again until just before the party tonight. She has plans with Ellie at the spa today. Only Ellie and Dave are in on our secret—other than Tina and Jonathan.

My golf game leaves something to be desired. I'm completely distracted thinking about tonight's celebration. I'm not even close to beating Emerson—not that I ever thought I had a chance. I was paired with three of our clients, and we tell terrible jokes and talk a lot of business.

"This is a brilliant idea for a company party," my client, Henry Blackwood, says as he pops a beer in the golf cart, and we talk about his new venture.

"We host one a year, and each one gets better than the last," I share.

"I'm not sure how you'll ever be able to beat this. My girlfriend wants to move into our hotel room, it's so plush and beautiful. We overlook the fountains and had a great view of the water and fireworks last night. She feels like she's been transported to France."

"Bella said something like that, too. Her plan today was to spend most of the day in the spa or the hotel bathroom."

"This hotel is going to be a huge success."

"I agree."

After lunch, I meet up with Maggie, Stevie, Hazel, and Richard. "Did Mother and Father make it?"

"Mother made a lame excuse. I know Jonathan would have loved to see them."

"Did you see Jonathan yet?"

Maggie blushes.

"He gave us a tour," Stevie shares. "This place is amazing. He has over three thousand rooms, and they are getting a permanent show for Lady Queen. Apparently, she's tired of traveling and wants to be with her kids."

"He's really done well for himself," I say, looking at Maggie. I know she always had a thing for him, but our parents were more interested in Alex since his parents own a giant electronics box store.

"How's Dad really doing?" I ask Maggie.

She shrugs. "They don't really talk about it. He was excited you told them you'd return to take over the business. I made sure they knew that Bella talked you into it."

"You do know that my plan is not to move back to Minnie, but between the three of us we'll hire a new CEO. I spoke to Emerson from my team and she has some of her best recruiters doing some preliminary looking."

"We can't hire anyone now," Stevie interjects.

"No way. I just want us to be able to move quickly when we do. I like the idea of a tech retailer CEO, possibly a founder of a smaller retail business. But I assure you, it will be a group decision."

Maggie and Stevie are happy with that.

"What's the big surprise tonight?"

"Well, we have the biggest band in the world doing a private show for us." I look at them both, only sharing half the secret. "Don't tell anyone though. We had Monkey Business last year and everyone went crazy."

"Are they signing autographs?"

I nod and put my finger to my lips. "It's a super secret or we'll have the entire strip breaking down the doors of Jonathan's new casino."

"This is going to be so much fun. This is the band you and I went to in Madison Square Garden."

I nod again. "You do realize you work for an amazing company. Your clients love you. We need to capture that for the stores."

"We will."

"I need to run. I need to get up to the room and get ready. They are letting me introduce Jonathan so I've got to look good."

I kiss my sister goodbye and get a half hug from Stevie.

We are almost ready to head to the Grand Ballroom.

"You know, not many people have over two hundred people at their elopement," I comment.

"Are you changing your mind?" Bella asks, looking concerned.

"Not in the least. I've wanted this since I told that creepy guy you were my fiancée."

She looks beautiful in her wedding dress with soft curls framing her face, but I can't wait to have her to myself in our room and naked.

We walk to the place where we've agreed to meet Tina behind the stage.

She greets us with a hug. "You both look great. I'm so excited. I'd like to introduce you to Tim Bradberry, your Elvis impersonator who's going to officiate your marriage.

"Very nice to meet you," he says, sounding just like Elvis. "This is my wife, Cindy, and she has some paperwork for you to fill out."

Just as we finish filling it out, Ellie and Dave join us.

I hear Ellie ask Bella, "Are you ready?"

Emerson finishes up awards and hands the microphone to Tina, who announces, "We have a special surprise. Christopher Reinhardt is going to make some introductions. For those of you who haven't met him, he works in our acquisitions teams in biotechnologies." There are some whoops from the audience.

Bella and I look at one another before making our way onto the stage. Elvis, Ellie, and Dave join us.

"Isn't this great being here at the Shangri-la? I don't know about you, but I think this is the most glamorous and beautiful hotel on the strip." The crowd whoops and hollers their agreement. "We are so lucky that they allowed us to showcase their skills on us before they officially open their doors. Let's put our hands together to thank Jonathan Best and his team." The crowd goes crazy for a solid two minutes.

I continue, "I grew up with Jonathan Best. He was this punk who was the smartest kid in our grade. When he called to tell me he was opening a hotel on the Las Vegas strip, I have to tell you, I didn't think he could pull this off. I've never been so glad to be wrong."

One of my clients yells from down below, "Good thing you didn't have his proposal go across your desk."

I laugh really hard. "You're right. For those of you in the back," and I repeat what was said. "But Jonathan has been amazing, and it's so great to have family and friends here together tonight. You may be wondering why I'm up here, and more importantly, why I've asked Elvis to join me. Well, the truth is he's up on stage to do something. You didn't realize that by being at the coolest party that Silicon Valley hosts each year, you were also being invited to a wedding tonight."

"Jesus, Mary, and Joseph," can be heard from the crowd.

"I think that was my future mother-in-law," I quip, and the crowd finally seems to understand.

"We'll let you get back to your party, but first, if you wouldn't mind being witnesses to our blessed event before the main event tonight."

The ballroom explodes in applause.

I hand the microphone to Elvis. "Ladies and gentlemen, thank you for joining Christopher and Isabella as they join their lives for now and forevermore." Looking at us, he says, "Isabella, please repeat after me. 'I, Isabella Maria Vargas, take you, Christopher Erickson Reinhardt, to be my husband, my partner in life, and my one true love. I will cherish our friendship and love you today, tomorrow, and forever.'"

Bella repeats her lines, and my heart swells with love.

• • •

"Christopher, please repeat after me. 'I, Christopher Erickson Reinhardt, take you, Isabella Maria Vargas, to be my wife, my partner in life, and my one true love. I will cherish our friendship and love you today, tomorrow, and forever.'"

I repeat my lines.

"Christopher, do you take Isabella to be your wife?"

"I do."

"Do you promise to love, honor, cherish, and protect her, forsaking all others and holding only unto her?"

"I do."

There is more whooping, and I think it's Stevie and Jonathan. I grin.

"Isabella, do you take Christopher to be your husband?"

"I do."

"Do you promise to love, honor, cherish, and protect him, forsaking all others and holding only unto him?"

"I do."

"Wedding rings are an unbroken circle of love, signifying to all the union of this couple in marriage."

He looks at me, and I know it's my turn. "Isabella, this ring is my sacred gift, with my promise that I will always love you, cherish you, and honor you all the days of my life. And with this ring, I thee wed." I slip a wedding band on her finger.

"Christopher, this ring is my sacred gift, with my promise that I will always love you, cherish you, and honor you all the days of my life. And with this ring, I thee wed." Isabella slips a platinum band on my left hand.

"By the power vested in me by the great State of Nevada, I now pronounce you husband and wife."

The crowd goes crazy, and Jonathan comes up to the stage, gives Bella and me a hug.

"This weekend has been a culmination of many years of planning. Thank you for being patient with us when we didn't have it down just right, and thanks everyone for helping to make the opening weekend and huge success." The crowd goes crazy. "It's my great pleasure to introduce you to the real reason you're here—Bono, The Edge, Adam Clayton, and Larry Mullen, Jr." The crowd goes completely crazy as U2 comes out on stage.

We walk off stage as Bono says, "For the bride and groom," and begins singing "It's a Beautiful Day."

As the partners and our families all descend on us, Bella says, "I hope you don't mind that we hijacked your party tonight."

"What? Are you kidding? This was awesome! Congratulations," Emerson says.

"But we didn't get to do a bachelorette party," CeCe bemoans.

"I didn't want one. I got the idea when I was trying on the wedding dresses. Mama, I know you want a big church wedding, and we can absolutely do one with Father Michael for just family."

"Oh, baby, I'm so happy for you both." She hugs us both and wipes tears from her eyes.

"Mother and Father are going to be so upset they missed this," Maggie announces.

"They can come to the church ceremony," I tell her. This was a great night, and I'm the happiest man on earth. "Thank you all for sharing it with us, and as much as we'd like to hear U2, we're heading upstairs to our suite to enjoy a quiet night of celebration."

"I hope it isn't too quiet," Dillon quips, and everyone laughs.

Read an excerpt

from:

Enchanted

Venture Capitalist Book 7

by Ainsley St Claire

(And, don't forget to sign-up for our newsletter/readers group. Don't miss a release or sale.)

chapter

ONE

QUINN

My other work phone is ringing. I check the caller ID before I answer. "Hello, handsome."

"What are you wearing?" he rasps into the phone.

"A black silk robe. I love the way it feels against my nipples." I breathe heavy for effect.

"Are you touching yourself?"

"I am. My pussy is wet. Can you hear me play with it? But what I want to know is if you are touching yourself?"

"My dick is so hard right now. What would you do if you were here with me?"

"Mmmmm… that's easy. I'd get down on my knees—" I pause for dramatic effect. "—then I'd lower the zipper to your jeans, and I hold on to your hard cock nice and tight." I moan my appreciation. "It's so big; I'm not sure I can take it all in my mouth. What should I do?"

"Take it deep in your mouth," he whimpers.

"Ohhh… my tongue swirls around the end. I love the way you taste."

"I want you to take it deeper in your throat."

"Can I play with my pussy at the same time?" I say in my best coquettish voice.

"Only if it's completely hairless."

"Smooth as a babies bottom. Tell me what you like. I want to please you."

"Play with your nipples and your pussy."

"Oh, that feels soooo good. Can you feel me take you deep in my throat?" I hear his breathing increase and I know he's close, but I don't want this to end yet. I whisper, "Don't come yet. I want to suck your balls."

He moans into the phone.

"I'm licking and sucking on your balls—swirling my tongue around and pulling gently."

"Pull harder," he commands.

"You get me so horny. My hand is so wet. I neeeeeed you."

"I want to hear you come for me."

"I'll only come for you if you will come all over my tits when I'm done."

"Jesus, woman, I don't think I've ever been this hard before."

I begin to moan my orgasm for him.

"Ahhh," he grunts into the phone. "Gawd, you're amazing. I can't sleep anymore without you. Are you working tomorrow night?"

I'm panting for added effect. "Yes."

"Can I call you again tomorrow?"

"I think I'll have recovered by then." I giggle seductively into the phone.

"Goodnight, Cinnamon."

"Goodnight, handsome. You'll haunt my dreams tonight."

He hangs up, and I walk into the kitchen, wearing sweatpants and a giant ratty old wool sweater I got years ago. I grab a Diet Coke from the fridge before my next client calls for his evening naughty talk.

Sitting down at my computer, I look at the project plan for my newest client. We've just invested almost two hundred million in a company who is working on a cure for Parkinson's Disease, and I'll oversee the office manager on-site and coordinate the recruiting and other operational sides of the business.

I pick up my phone, and it lights up, showing I've been on the phone with one of the partners for over a half hour. I quickly push the red button to disconnect the call. Fuck! I'd called William to leave him a message about his newest client and what he was trying to accomplish when my second job phone rang. I thought I'd disconnected the call. Crap.

Living in San Francisco is expensive. My one-bedroom apartment has a rent more than most people's mortgage, and I don't have a parking space or washer and dryer, and my view is of the street outside of my third-floor walk-up. Plus, I have a school loan payment of over four thousand dollars a month. I'm drowning in debt, so I took a second job that didn't require me to have strange people get in and out of my car or actually prostitute my body out to strange men—eww! I've gotten to know men too well doing the job, but they don't know my actual name and only think they know what I look like from the highly photoshopped picture. I make a dollar a minute plus tips, which means over eight hours I earn about two hundred and fifty dollars a night, and I try to work at least six nights a week. It pays my school loans and puts a dent in my rent, but it's often lonely. I haven't been out with my friends for so long they've stopped asking.

My phone rings again.

"Hello, handsome."

"Cinnamon, do you have some time to talk?"

"Jeffery?"

"Oh, sorry. Yes, this is Jeffery."

"Of course. What's wrong?"

"My company is going public, and I'm freaking out. I just need to hear the calm in your voice to get me off the ledge."

"I'm here for you, baby. Just imagine me cuddled up next to you."

"I love how soft your breasts are."

"You're so naughty when you play with my nipples." I moan into the phone. "I'll promise to stroke that beautiful cock, but only if you tell me what's bothering you."

He goes through the litany of challenges that he's facing. I want to tell him he should have invested with my company SHN, but first that would be too close to home, and second, I'm not exactly sure who Jeffery is, but I don't really want to find out.

• • •

Most of my job is to listen to the men who call. Some want to have a physical release when they talk to me, and others just need a sympathetic ear. Jeffery keeps me on the phone for over three hours, and when we hang up, I get a message that he's tipped me five hundred dollars. A good night. I turn my phone off and stop taking calls.

My mind drifts back to my open call with William. I've never wanted my professional job to intersect with my second job. They should never mix.

The bile rises in my throat. I don't know what I'm going to do.

Okay, there are two possibilities. I said goodbye, and he hangs up, and most likely he never listens to all of my messages. Or he listens and tells everyone, and not only am I beyond embarrassed but I'll most likely lose my job, and then I'm in serious trouble with my bills.

Fuckity, fuck, fuck, fuck! I can't believe I was careless. Shit.

What am I going to do? How am I going to explain this to him?

What if he thinks I was talking to him? Oh, gawd! I run my hand through my hair, and I see several strands laced in my fingers, and now I'm sure the stress is making my hair fall out, and I'm going to go bald. Why can't anything be easy?

I have an idea. Maybe I can go in and erase the message. I search "How to erase voice mail messages on someone else's cell phone."

Shit! I'm not a hacker.

Okay. Think, Quinn. Do you know anyone who can hack a phone?

No one.

Cameron from work—maybe? But then I'd have to explain to him why I need him to break into William's phone.

Breathe.

All right. What did I say to the caller?

Think.

I told him how I liked how my nipples feel against silk. *Shit! I'm screwed.*

I'm sure he's the type of guy who would erase the message after I said, "Goodbye." He may not have even listened to the message to that point.

I hope. I pace my small living room and bite at the nail on my thumb. How can I ever go back to work again? What am I going to say when I see him? Can I avoid him for the rest of my life?

Quinn, how could you've been so stupid?

chapter

TWO

WILLIAM

I roll over half asleep and say, "Alexa, alarm off." I cover my eyes and desperately want to go back to sleep, but it's five, and I need to work out. Pulling on a pair of shorts and tucking my feet in my running shoes, I walk to my home gym in my condo. It's really the second bedroom, but I don't have guests, so I have a decent treadmill that I run on each day as I look out on the Golden Gate Bridge. Sometimes, if I feel up for it, I may go for a run up and down the boardwalk, but this time of year there are too many tourists, and it's just easier to run inside.

Noticing a missed a call from last night, I pop my cell phone into the cradle for the speaker on the side table and push play on the message. Once the message is over it will move over to my music. Setting the treadmill for a four-minute mile, I jump on and start running. I love how it clears my head and sets me up for a good day.

"Hey, William. It's Quinn. I met with the team at Worldwide Payments and have a timeline all set up. I think we'll be good with one operations person who can double with our help on the recruiting side. I also"—I can hear a phone ring in the background—"think we may need to look at some of the support staff. Let's talk about it in the morning. Goodnight."

I wait for the call to disconnect, but it doesn't.

Then I hear her, in the sweetest, most sultry, southern drawl. "Hello, handsome."

I almost trip over my feet. It's quiet a moment, and then I hear her describe giving the guy a blow job. Before I fall off the treadmill, I stop it and walk up to the speaker. She isn't talking into the phone's microphone, so I can barely hear her, but I know exactly what she's saying. Her voice is so fucking hot. And since I know what she looks like, I wonder what it would be like to have her going down on me.

Holy fucking shit! My cock could pound nails right now it's so hard.

I know I should disconnect the call and erase the voice mail, but I'm so aroused I can't bring myself to do it. I listen for the entire length of the call, and she finally tells whomever she's talking to "Goodbye," I can't help but stroke myself.

Who could she have been talking to? A boyfriend? I've never had phone sex like that, but I'd sure like to.

I'm not in any serious relationship. I have a few girls I see when I need a date or want some fun, but no one who talks to me like that.

She disconnects from the call, and I then hear her hum the sweetest melody.

• • •

I've always thought Quinn was stunning. She's blonde, with an incredible rack and legs that I wouldn't mind wrapped around my waist while I pounded into her. Okay, I only thought that last part since I heard her talking on the phone. I don't mix my personal life with my professional life, so I try to only admire my female colleagues from afar.

Holy crap. How will I ever look at her again and not have a huge hard-on?

I glance at the clock, and unless I get a move on, I'm going to be late for work.

The water is warm as I ease myself into the shower, and I keep replaying her sultry voice saying, "I want to please you." I begin to stroke myself until I shower the wall with my orgasm.

How am I going to be able to get through the day and not want to bend her over my desk and pound her hard from behind?

As I walk into the office, I can't help but look around for her. I don't see her. She has a cubicle on the other side of the office, and we rarely interact.

I finally spot her. Her hair is up in a ponytail—easier to pull her deeper on my cock, I think as I fantasize about her.

She's wearing a black turtleneck sweater and black pants with a pair of sexy stilettos—I wonder what her underwear looks like? I wonder, if I were to tweak her nipples, would she moan in appreciation or knee me in the balls? Probably the latter.

I need to get my mind out of the gutter. I need to forget the message and focus on Worldwide Payments. My deal has been funded, and the goal is to finalize the software with Cameron's team over the next year and prepare to take them public. Without Quinn's help, my deal with go south, and not only will the company be out of their investment, but I'll be out of a job.

• • •

She did leave a message saying we would talk about my issue today. I'd also like to include Mason, Cameron, and possibly someone from his team to do some planning. I check everyone's calendars and send out an invite for a meeting tomorrow afternoon to discuss.

As I push send, I look over in Quinn's direction. I watch her pop up and look at me. I glimpse a pink flush cover her face, and even that makes me hard. I look away.

What is this woman doing to me?

THANK YOU!

I can't tell you how much it means to me that you've given me the time to share with you the stories that ramble around in my head. This is a dream come true for me to be allowed to introduce you to a group of people that are my friends. If you like it well enough, feel free to write a review on your favorite review site - you can find me on Amazon, Goodreads, and Bookbub. If you want to know the exact date, know what's going on with my books join my newsletter. I try to send only one a month but if I'm releasing a book, you might get a second.

Other people to thank include my amazing husband. He's my inspiration for Christopher (only his family are potato farmers and not department store moguls ;)). But in his pure kindness and willingness to go two-hundred miles above and beyond for Bella is purely based on him. He's my muse and my always.

My editors from Hot Tree Editing are amazing. My content editor Barbara really helped to keep me on track. I had a big spoiler in this book and she caught it and suggested I take it out. So you can blame her. ;) All in good time! Virginia did the heavy lifting with this book and my line edit. She makes sure all those commas and apostrophe's are in the right place. I take great comfort in knowing that one of my all-time favorite authors, Ernst Hemingway is known for not having used any punctuation in his manuscripts and drove his editors crazy. Granted, I'm no Hemingway, but I assure you Virginia has all her hair still on her head. I also have a fabulous final editor Kim and Clara and Sue, my wonderful beta readers who always find the last few missing periods, commas, and things that don't make sense.

Aria Tran at Resplendent Media does an outstanding jobs with my covers. I adore her and all her work. I highly recommend her!

And to my friends, Gayle, Erin, Carol, Jocelyn, Julie, Nicky, and Nicole, THANK YOU! These ladies listen to me talk unending about my books, let me talk through the plot points that sounded so good when I mapped out the series and now make no sense as I'm writing. You girls are my biggest fans and greatest support. Thank you for listening even when I'm pretty sure you're over me talking about it.

I'm off to figure out the next cocktail for my next book. Hmm…vodka, rum, bourbon, or gin base? I'll let you know!

Thanks again!

XOXO

A.

WHERE TO FIND AINSLEY

If you are interested in sneak peaks, random cocktail recipes that show up in my stories, or just the simple reminder to read the next book in the series, please join my reading group:

www.ainsleystclaire.com

Join Ainsley's newsletter

Follow Ainsley on Bookbub

Like Ainsley St Claire on Facebook

Join Ainsley's Naughty Readers group

Follow Ainsley St Claire on Twitter

Follow Ainsley St Claire on Goodreads

Visit Ainsley's website for her current booklist

I love to hear from you directly, too. Please feel free to email me at ainsley@ainsleystclaire.com or check out my website www.ainsleystclaire.com for updates.

ALSO BY AINSLEY ST CLAIRE

Forbidden Love (Venture Capitalist Book 1) Available on Amazon
(Emerson and Dillon's story) He's an eligible billionaire. She's off limits. Is a relationship worth the risk?

Promise (Venture Capitalist Book 2) Available on Amazon
(Sara and Trey's story) She's reclaiming her past. He's a billionaire dodging the spotlight. Can a romance of high achievers succeed in a world hungry for scandal?

Desire (Venture Capitalist Book 3) Available on Amazon
(Cameron and Hadlee's story) She used to be in the 1%. He's a self-made billionaire. Will one hot night fuel love's startup?

Temptation (Venture Capitalist Book 4) Available on Amazon
(Greer and Andy's story) She helps her clients become millionaires and billionaires. He transforms grapes into wine. Can they find more than love at the bottom of a glass?

Obsession (Venture Capitalist Book 5) Available on Amazon
(Cynthia and Todd's story) With hitmen hot on their heels, can Cynthia and Todd keep their love alive before the mob bankrupts their future?

Flawless (Venture Capitalist Book 6) Available on Amazon
(Constance and Parker's story) A woman with a secret. A tech wizard on the trail of hackers. A tycoon's dying revelation threatens everything.

Longing (Venture Capitalist Book 7) Available on Amazon
(Bella and Christopher's story) She's a biotech researcher in race with time for a cure. If she pauses to have a life, will she lose the race? He needs a deal to keep his job. Can they find a path to love?

Enchanted (Venture Capitalist Book 8) Available for PreOrder on Amazon
(Quinn and William's Story) Women don't hold his interest past a week, until she accidentally leaves me a voice mail so hot it melts his phone. I need a fake fiancée for one week. What can a week hurt?

In a Perfect World Available on Amazon
Soulmates and true love. They believed in it once… back when they were twenty. As college students, Kat Moore and Pete Wilder meet and unknowingly change their lives forever. Despite living on opposite sides of the country, they develop a love for one another that never seems to work out. (Women's fiction)

COMING SOON

Gifted (A Holiday Story)
November 2019

ABOUT AINSLEY

Ainsley St Claire is a Contemporary Romantic Suspense Author and Adventurer on a lifelong mission to craft sultry storylines and steamy love scenes that captivate her readers. To date, she is best known for her Venture Capitalist series.

An avid reader since the age of four, Ainsley's love of books knew no genre. After reading, came her love of writing, fully immersing herself in the colorful, impassioned world of romantic suspense.

Ainsley's passion immediately shifted to a vocation when during a night of terrible insomnia, her first book came to her. Ultimately, this is what inspired her to take that next big step. The moment she wrote her first story, the rest was history.

When she isn't being a bookworm or typing away her next story on her computer, Ainsley enjoys spending quality family time with her loved ones. She is happily married to her amazing soulmate and is a proud mother of two rambunctious boys. She is also a scotch aficionada and lover of good food (especially melt-in-your-mouth, velvety chocolate). Outside of books, family, and food, Ainsley is a professional sports spectator and an equally as terrible golfer and tennis player.

Made in the USA
Coppell, TX
21 November 2020